Darlin

Loves In Time, Volume 3

Jewel Adams

Published by JA Creations, 2022.

First edition. January 26, 2022.

Copyright © 2022 Jewel Adams.

ISBN: 979-8201542160

Written by Jewel Adams.

Table of Contents

Darlin

Book 3 in the Loves in Time series
Time Travel Sensual Romance

Flint is ready to give the brat fighting him to the Indians as he pushes the lad over the next waterfall. Once rinsed of mud, he discovers the frail boy is one nicely shaped woman. Learning his employer intends to marry off the girl, his Darlin', with the indentured women, he marries her himself suspecting he has gone from the frying pan and into the fire.

Marrying Allen Flint isn't as disturbing to Jolene as discovering she is in 1713. Dare she examine her feelings toward the mountain of a man, now a part of her life? Can she survive the wilds of the American Frontier?

When Indians capture Flint, Jolene prays she possesses the strength to save the man she loves from certain death. Time brought her to him, but Jolene realizes only their magic can hold them together, now.

Prologue

"Alright, which one of you put her up to it?" Jolene glared at her friends. The denial floated through the car.

Mary Joe leaned forward from the backseat. "Well, I sure didn't. It wasn't fair that you monopolized the whole séance, Jolene."

"Not by choice." Flicking the auburn wisps back behind her ear, Jolene's brow creased again recalling the strange evening.

Jean dropped off Lynn and Mary Joe first, before driving back to her house where Jolene left her car.

"Why so quiet, Joe? You don't really believe all that mumbo jumbo?"

"No, of course not." But her answer sounded weak. "Why would she say something so off the wall like that?"

"Probably wanted to make an impression on us so we'd send her more business."

"Yes, you're right." But did she have to scare her in the process? What did she say when they were leaving? *Beware of what kills in silence.*

Rubbing her arms, the goose bumps had little to do with the warm summer night. After saying goodnight to Jean, Jolene tried to forget the unsettling events of the evening. She didn't believe in such nonsense. So why couldn't she forget the woman's words?

Halfway home a roll of thunder vibrated through the car. Already upset, Joe scolded herself for going. "I'd be home by now and not out in a summer downpour."

Just as her words fell silent, huge drops of rain splattered the windshield. She searched for the wiper switch as her foot went to the brake. When the wipers flew across the windshield, she felt the tension ease out of her shoulders. She needed to lean forward to see the white line in the middle of the road, nearly missing her mailbox and the turn up the mountain to her home.

"I should have listened to Jean and rented old Teran's place in town instead of living out here." Shaking her head she knew she couldn't give up her grandfather's cabin. It had always been her home and would remain so. She loved her mountain.

At the sharp curve, she just came about the side when she saw the fallen tree across the road and slammed on the brakes. The car careened into the large tree trunk, throwing her forward over the impact. It took all her strength to bring her head off the steering wheel. She groaned as she raised her hands to hold the vicious throb at her temple. Sitting there Jolene fought off the dizzy sensation folding in on her. She started shaking all over, but only her head held pain, a sharp throbbing assault.

The storm gave no sign of letting up. Living her whole life at the threshold of the Smoky Mountains she knew this was an all nighter. Straining to see past her blurry vision the dashboard finally came into focus, *eleven thirty-four.* The prospect of sitting in the car all night ended over the ache in her head. She needed to get home. It was only half a mile up the road, a road no one else ever came up.

Jolene tried to get her purse off the floor, but the effort made her winch. She would get it tomorrow. She made sure everything was turned off then pocketed the keys in her jeans, wishing she'd thought to bring an umbrella. The sound of heavy rain hitting the hood in angry pulses, told her it wouldn't have helped tonight.

Counting to three didn't give her enough time to build up her courage so she sat there and counted to ten. Jolene pushed the door open against the storm's wind and the branches that fell around the car.

Fighting her way through the limbs, her blouse became soaked by the time she reached the tree trunk. She didn't have the strength to pull herself over it. Getting down on her knees she crawled along the fallen tree until she found a gap wide enough to slide under. The road bed turned into mud, and she grimaced as she edged under the trunk. Once away from the fallen tree her head hurt so much she just laid there, letting the rain plummet her backside. She wanted to sleep, but the little voice of sanity told her to get up and make it to the cabin.

It took several tries before she came fully to her feet. The mud sucked at her loafers until Jolene wasn't sure if she still wore them. All around her the storm raged, lightening flashed in ugly jagged scars, but the thunder filled her, its roaring vibration went on, stealing her breath away.

Stumbling, she fell. Lying there she felt the ground shake beneath her. "Oh no, not thunder!"

She frantically looked all around her, feeling the panic rise as the rumbling beneath her body increased. Using every bit of strength at her command, Jolene pushed to her feet to run, but feared she would run into the flash flood. She tried to clear the rivulets of water from her eyes and search the darkness, knowing that at any second, the terror would burst out upon her.

When it came, Jolene's screams were lost in the rush of mud and water bombarding her. Over and over she rolled, carried by the sheet of moving earth. She felt so odd, almost detached from the fury, as if she couldn't really feel anything...except her fear, and the deluge became her world, swallowing her up in the terror, until everything crashed down about her in a deafening swirl of darkness.

CHAPTER 1
Wild Ride

"**D**amn savages." Using his elbows Flint soundlessly pulled himself into the thick underbrush. Never once did he lose track of the large hunting party skirting the far edge of the meadow. They were headed west with no guarantee they hadn't already spotted the wagons. Maybe he should turn back and warn them?

Judging the distance to the east between them, Flint decided it made more sense to keep going west to Fort Pratt. He'd just have some unwanted company for a little while. At least he'd know if they were meeting another group and their true intent.

Staying downwind from the Cree, Flint moved to the pace they set, not liking it much that they were headed in exactly his direction. He didn't like bringing the wagons into the Cherokee Territory riddled with Indian trouble, but that stubborn Scotsman wouldn't listen to his advice. Flint knew the reason the man wanted to go to the Fort and it still bothered him. Right now he'd like to give Mathew Fergusson a good lashing for ever getting him involved with tracking for the self-serving McKean.

Brushing away his ire over the man, he needed all wits about him at the moment to play this dangerous game of tag, one slip and it could turn deadly.

More confused than she ever remember being, Jolene sat heavily on the inviting log. Pulling at her shirt she tried to shake off the dried mud that now turned the white blouse a reddish brown. Curling her lip up over how filthy she felt, she gave up the effort. Being dirty seemed the least of her problems since coming around...this morning?

Gingerly touching the bruise at her forehead, she whispered, "How long was I out?"

It was daylight and because her jeans were still drying, she felt safe in concluding it must only be the next morning. She shuddered, recalling the flash flood.

What she didn't have any answers for, is exactly where she ended up. "Lost...*The obvious is always easy, Jolene.*" Repeating her grandfather's favorite saying didn't take away the ill feeling that started once her head cleared a bit. There hadn't been a familiar landmark anywhere. When she failed to locate the car or cabin it became obvious the slide took her a lot farther than she first imagined. She'd roamed these mountains all through her childhood. There wasn't a nook or cranny within ten miles of the cabin that she didn't know. So where the frig' was she?

By her calculations, after deciding to head downhill, she'd gone at least two miles. It would be practically impossible not to stumble across some private dirt road, even a fire break or utility lines, something should have shown up.

Knowing how bad she ached, the thought of moving again made her hold her mud caked head. Touching the muck clinging to her hair made her want to laugh, but the effort would hurt too much. She'd probably scare the first person she came across.

At first Jolene didn't pay any attention to the low sounds. But when the movement caught her gaze she grew stiff. Never rising off the log, she slowly parted the branches of a mountain laurel and cautiously leaned forward for a better look. "I'm hallucinating."

Flint's senses snapped to attention over the sound. *What the hell!* If the boy hadn't spoken out, Flint would have moved right past him.

Quickly looking at his other unwanted companions he let his breath out in slow deliberation. They hadn't heard the kid. Damn fool, the boy should know better living in these parts. By the grubby look of him he wasn't a greenhorn.

Ready to dismiss the boy and move on, Flint's heated curse never passed his lips when he realized the boy's intention. Moving without thinking and the urgency driving him, Flint held only one conviction, *when this was over that boy would get a what-for he'd never forget!*

Jolene decided they must be Cherokee. It must be some re-enactment or something for the tourists. The thought raised her hopes. At least they could help her get back to civilization. That hit on her head must have muddled her sense of direction. Rising to call them before they disappeared into the woods... "Hey!"

The vicious curse behind the rough hold pulling her to the ground shocked her into silence. The large hand covering her mouth smothered her stunned expletives.

"You stupid little fool!"

Indignation welled up in a furious torrent inside Jolene.

"Come on!"

The man yanked her to her feet, knocking the breath out of her. The violent jerk on her arm dragged her uselessly backwards across the ground. Being forcibly pulled when she already hurt so terribly made her madder than a cat in water! She managed to gain her clumsy footing, but failed to shake off the iron clasp on her wrist. Running and catching up to the thick leather clad legs in front of her, Jolene reached out to claw at the breaking grip his massive fingers kept on her arm. "Let go!"

Growling at the man only made him jerk her up beside him. Nearly lifting her off her feet he hissed at her, "Shut up, before I let them have you!"

The threat came through chillingly clear even in her rattled condition. Pressing her lips tight, Jolene let her fuming rage lend strength into the flight the monster forced her maintain. Crashing through bushes, jumping rocks, unable to see what might come next, she put all her concentration on his powerful legs. Their next movement told her what to prepare for. *God, they are so big!*

Swallowing back a moan, she realized what kind of man held her, but Jolene didn't have time to give in to the deserved panic knotting her battered body. Coming to an abrupt halt she plowed into him with the force of their inertia. His vile curses sent her cheeks flaming, but the great strength in his hands stilled her heated retort. Heavens, he could crush her without a thought!

"Get going!"

"What?" Looking where he suddenly pointed, her violet eyes grew two sizes over what she saw. Shaking her head in violent denial made her groan over the pain she caused herself. The open expanse of air before her made her gulp. The sheer slope of stones at her feet made her back into the solid wall of rock-solid muscle.

"Start sliding down!"

Her disbelieving eyes glared at him as she backed away from both threats. Jolene knew exactly where she was, Devil Falls. Nature's thrill ride down the water slick rocks into the pools below. Maybe some people thought it was fun, but Jolene held little interest in this sick joy ride.

He moved so fast she didn't have time to react, her squeal filled the air as he pushed her down onto the rocks. Before she could get up, those awesome legs came about her waist locking her in a human vise.

"No way! You are crazy!"

"You're going to find out just how much so!" When the push came sending them forward to go over the falls, so did his hold on her hair.

Closing her eyes, the ride picked up speed as they rode the smooth curving slopes and skimmed over the rocks. The water carried them on, hitting them like a thousand tiny icicles as it splashed all around them. Roller coasters held nothing on this! The threat of losing her stomach over the sinking ups and downs, kept her jaw clenched and the screams sounding only in her head.

"Hold your breath!"

His warning wasn't necessary, she'd never let it out.

The shock of dropping into the mountain chilled pool at first stunned her, then adrenaline shot through her veins. Jolene didn't need any shove to start swimming, she wanted to escape this maniac. The man's continued hold on her hair made her aim a few well-placed kicks at his solid mass beside her.

Flint grunted. The boy kicked him in the gut. Maybe he should have let them have this boy! Why he was fighting mad at Flint made no sense. With a powerful grip, he pulled the boy beneath the water to cool his fire.

Gasping for breath, Jolene clung to the first thing her hands locked onto. "I'll kill you, you bastard!"

"Now son, I'd save all that anger for them...you'll need it."

God, he was actually laughing at her!

"Over you go!" His hand covered her rump to push.

Jolene took all she could of his insolence and lashed out with some strong, lowdown remarks. "...take your vile hands off me." Grinding out her threat through the wet veil of hair, she didn't expect his next attack.

Gripping her jaw he forced her head away from him. "You want to stay and face that, so be it."

She blinked. How could...? Why? The arrow embedded in the log by her head was still quivering from its deadly flight...*beware of what kills in silence.*

She felt him rise out of the water, then slide over the rock. When his outstretched hand filled her stunned vision, Jolene no longer hesitated.

The next slide she took on her stomach, thankful that it wasn't as long as the first.

Two more times she followed him blindly through the pools and next natural slide, until the last one sent them falling in the rapids of the rushing river.

His powerful hand wrapped tight in her hair was the only thing that kept her from being pulled under the rushing water. How long the terrifying ride in the current lasted she didn't dare think about, all Jolene knew was she didn't want to drown. Somewhere, through her fear she admitted this man was the only thing that kept her from doing so.

She didn't realize they were out of the water until the cold, gritty bank lay beneath her out-stretched body. Taking deep revitalizing breaths, her gaze fell on the enormous feet sprawled beside her.

"Get up boy, they aren't giving up."

Pushing up with her elbow she shook her head to clear away the weakness and the crazy thoughts assaulting her. Was this some weird nightmare or was she really hallucinating? Shock sounded reasonable for what she felt.

Lifting the lad up by his shirt Flint set him on his...bare feet! Damn, he'd have to think of something, the boy's feet wouldn't last long running over this rock jagged terrain. The boy showed gumption, making Flint question the frailty he felt against his brawn. They were losing their lead on those Cree.

This was one big man. Seeing his full height coming to life before her, Jolene didn't have the will left to keep her eyes from looking over his glorious build.

Broad as a tree, came unbidden to her thoughts, but lean in tough unyielding strength. She tried to force her gaze away from the flat trim hips and waist. Through the clinging wet leather that molded to his ample frame she sucked in her breath over the display of ripcord muscles. The open vee at his neck said he'd be sleek all over. The unbidden impression made her wondered how big he was...well *there*.

Nearly groaning when her eyes jumped down to see, she forced herself not to look. Swallowing hard, Jolene tried not to think too much on how he would look naked.

Big, very, very big! She couldn't believe she was thinking thoughts like this...now! She looked up and followed the powerful line of his neck, "My word!"

Wet and hanging in golden curls, his hair framed the most exquisite male face she'd ever set eyes on. Handsome didn't come close to the raw sensuality he exhibited. Thank God his attention wasn't on her, but how she wished she could see the color of his eyes. The straight set of his nose in those high cheek bones and square jaw lent an air of authority to his commanding presence.

"Boy! I said we need to fix you up some shoes for..." But Flint forgot his intent as his eyes raced up the slim frame, coming to an abrupt halt over the white transparent cloth sticking to the very real...womanly breasts!

His jaw worked furiously over the stark evidence of what he'd failed to notice. Rinsed of the mud he blamed for blinding his sight and senses, he saw them now, and they were in full awareness! The frail boy was one nicely shaped, if not soaked, woman.

Jolene silently agreed with the heated curse hissing out of the man's full lips. Her awareness of this handsome and strong man proved just as shocking. His eyes were as blue as a deep lake on a winter day, yes, any other color would not work as nicely. God, she could drown in their heat... *Ach!*

When his potent lips eased before her, Jolene had to shake herself out of her blatant study of him. Seeing exactly where his gaze rested brought her arms up in a decidingly defensive measure, folding them firmly across her chest.

Flint silently groaned. If she realized the effect her action struck against his heightened senses, the way the sweet roundness of her breasts pressed up against the material in such abandon... Snapping his gaze away, his awareness of the present dangers stalking them practically kicked him hard enough to take away his breath. The threat in her stormy gaze did more to cool him than their dunks in the mountain pools. He wasted no more time.

When he pulled his shirt up and over his head, Jolene's arms dropped and her feet tensed for flight. But when he took out his huge knife and cut away the bottom half of the shirt her curiosity kept her rooted to the spot. Seeing the full rippling evidence of his massive shoulders left her knees shaking. His body reflected copper and bronze, he reeked of pure unadulterated power!

When he lifted her foot, she automatically grasped his steeled shoulder to keep from falling.

"The moss will help soften the rocks."

Captured by the heat infusing her sensitive fingertips, she almost missed his meaning over the makeshift shoes.

As he rose to his full height before her, Jolene almost fell back following his progress. His hand reached out towards her face her eyes closed in slow apprehension. She snapped her eyes open at the surprising gentle brush of his fingers on the sore bruise on her brow. Biting her lip, she stopped herself from leaning into his strength.

"Will you be able to run?"

Answer him Jolene, before he thinks you are an idiot. "Yes, I think so."

Nodding at her answer Flint didn't miss one nuance of her behavior, unfortunately his own reaction to her wasn't much better. What Flint didn't like was the ugly darkness at her temple. She hadn't gotten it during their escape. No, it wouldn't be that dark yet. It was a wonder she could stand at all. What they still faced ahead of them made every nerve in his body rise in concern. The prospect of failing and what she'd face in those savages' hands brought on a rage so intense Flint thought he could kill them all bare handed. If need be he'd give it one hell of a try!

CHAPTER 2
Discovery

Grinding her teeth together, Jolene suffered in silence. She kept telling herself not to look away from his legs, knowing it would mean falling again. But, her head wouldn't stop throbbing and each running step made the pounding more intense.

She wanted to cry out and make him stop, but his last words to her forbade the weakness. As if to confirm their meaning her fingers felt for the large knife he'd stuck into her belt.

"If they get us...use it." No, she'd not mistaken the cold meaning as his gaze touched her face, she knew exactly what act he wanted her to commit and it made the bile rise and tighten her throat. This couldn't be happening.

Her denial faded the deeper they ran into the mountains. The grueling distance made it very real. She may have missed a road or a house before, but Jolene finally started to figure out her location. They were headed southwest, even if they somehow managed not to cross it, she felt positive she should see the Blue Ridge parkway. She kept scanning the massive mountains each time they topped another rise...nothing!

Worse, there had been nothing to lend credence to the civilization she knew should be in the hollows and open valleys. Maybe she feared the answers she'd get if she asked the man anything. Because of the threat still following them, neither of them spoke. He used hand signals to tell her when she could rest. Jolene realized each time he left her he went to check and see if they were still being followed. She refused to think what she might do if he didn't come back. She didn't even know his name...

Flint heard her slight whimper, cursing the cause. For such a little thing she sure carried around a lot of stamina. She didn't complain, not once, but Flint could see the pain etched across her face. No longer were her eyes that clear blue violet. They were glassed over to fight the pain she kept silent, leaving them almost gray.

The Cree braves weren't giving up, damn them. They were being forced further south, no matter how hard he tried to veer back west. When he back-tracked this time, if they were any closer Flint would have to head east and hope he could lose them. It meant leaving her. He didn't have any choice she couldn't take anymore of this grueling pace.

He sensed the change in her, turning he grabbed hold of her to keep her from colliding into him. Flint felt her sway before she went limp. He gently lifted her up in his arms and started to search for somewhere to hide her.

Placing her carefully into a group of bushes, he pushed the leaves over her tiny body. Squatting down beside her he surveyed his handiwork, satisfied they'd have to fall over her to find her. He brushed back the reddish wisps of hair from her face. "Now, my Darlin', stay quiet and they won't find you."

He actually held his breath as those thick lashes of gold fluttered open. Flint sucked in his breath over the smile she looked up at him with. "I'll be back when I've led them away, Darlin'. Don't move or make a sound."

Jolene liked this strange man, his eyes were so soft. "I don't think you have to worry about that."

"You did good, Darlin'."

"I'm sorry, my head hurts so."

Flint's finger gently caressed the dark bruise. He wished there was time to help her. "I'm going to draw them east."

Before he could rise, her small fingers grasped his arm and stilled his leave.

"Not east, there is a deep ravine, you'll be trapped. Go south through the next hollow, it will lead you around the cliffs. There will be a meadow, you can head east through the pass. Half way down is a cave, you really have to look for the entrance. If you find it you could hide there until they pass." The directions exhausted the last of her strength.

"Don't go anywhere Darlin'," he said patting her hand.

She gave him a small hurting laugh. "What's your name?"

"Flint." She started drifting off, he barely heard her.

"...like my mountains."

He forced himself to pull his gaze away from her face as her eyes closed. Covering her with the last of the leaves, Flint worked his way back from where she laid hidden, hiding all evidence of their presence.

Taking off in a run, he made sure he left tracks. He wondered how long they'd follow him before they noticed her absence. Flint didn't like leaving her, but the alternative meant sure failure. Using the girl's directions, he moved with confidence through the terrain. He now held speed on his side, but he couldn't get her out of his mind.

Noise? Yes, there it was again. Coming full awake, Jolene tried to concentrate past the roaring in her head. *Don't move, don't breathe.* The remembered warnings sent shivers over her, the cold felt like it came from deep in her bones.

She sensed their presence before she saw them through the brush. Jolene tasted the blood on her lip as she bit down with the force she used not to cry out.

Their dark bare skin glistened in the late afternoon sun, contrasting sharply with the vivid streaks of paint on their faces and chests. The red, black and yellow marks made them look fierce. The large blades and clubs hanging from their waists held every bit of danger she felt by their menacing manner. There were five. Jolene watched without moving as they searched the ground.

Was Flint safe? How far ahead would he be by now? She'd lost track of time.

The sudden raised timber of their voices drew her attention back to them. Her panic rose to a dangerous level over the argument taking place before her. She didn't need a translation to know two of them were angry over the tracks. A single where two once walked?

Jolene closed her eyes and wished she could truly disappear. She didn't want to think of the reason they spoke in such an odd tongue. Why not English or Cherokee? No, these men weren't Cherokee, and they weren't like any of the Indians she personally knew lived around here.

Forcing her attention back to them, she felt relieved to see the majority won. Though the way two of the braves hung back and scanned the ground, she didn't think they were all that convinced. The troubled thought wouldn't leave her that they would be back once their suspicions were confirmed. If they did come back they wouldn't stop looking until they found her.

Searching the ground near her, her hand closed over a palm sized rock. Being careful not to make any more noise than the leaves falling away at her movement, she lofted the rock away from her position. Calling on every sense and nerve, she waited to see if any of the men responded to the noise.

Praying they weren't lying in wait for her to move, Jolene struggled to her knees. Dizzy and weak she shivered under a seizing chill. She fought to stand, and then Jolene moved deliberately out into the open. Seconds dragged on as she waited for the attack that never came.

"Must lead them away..." Only a short trail to the ravine, then she would double back over the rocks.

Getting to the precipice took longer than she'd realized. Her unsteady gait made it difficult. Holding onto a tree she kicked at the dirt edge with her heel until it broke away. *Come on girl, all those years of learning to hide from Jerry Gilliam can't fail you now.*

However she found the strength, she wouldn't question its presence. Jolene pulled herself up by a branch and finally managed to place her feet securely on the boulder. Dropping to her knees she began the long course back over the rocks.

Fighting away the darkness trying to overtake her, Jolene filled her thoughts with the large man called Flint. If the ploy didn't work she would be finished. By the time she reached the boulder, above her forsaken hiding place, she knew she could go no farther.

The darkness came and the full moon illuminated the open area below her perch.

Braced between the rocks she waited, wanting to see only one large shadow appear.

Jolene refused to give into the raging fever now full upon her.

How the hell did she know about the cave? The opening was practically invisible. Flint almost gave up his search for it. If those bats hadn't come out at dusk, he never would have located it. Once their horde vacated the cave, Flint took up his spot. From here he could see in both directions.

At the end of his patience, he was ready to start back when they finally appeared. "...two, three, four...where the hell is the last one?"

Flint's body stiffened over the answer and commanded himself to stay hidden. As he hoped, they followed the trail he staked out. It would take them another half a mile. He didn't have much time to reach her. What he didn't like were his thoughts over the missing Cree brave.

Under the moon Flint moved over the trail, always on alert for whatever danger could be waiting in the shadows. Nearing the area where he'd left the woman, Flint moved into the woods, deciding to take a different approach. An uneasy stillness sent the hairs up on his neck in warning. The Cree brave was close, he could feel him and the rage inside Flint flared stronger.

The Indian stood directly below her, moving the bed of leaves with his foot. As she'd feared one of them did come back and scoured the area until he found her empty hiding place. Jolene cursed the darkness that kept him from seeing her tracks to the ravine. The fever brought on chills in a dry torrent. Staying conscious became more difficult. She feared her painful sobs wouldn't remain silent if she gave into the nothingness trying to swallow her. If only she could move to stay awake, but he prevented the luxury.

A violent fury raged through Flint when he finally located the brave. Realizing the savage's actions meant the woman was no longer there stilled his attack. He hoped it also meant she remained safe. Decisions came quickly in the wilds, delays met with destruction.

Watching him a second longer, Flint moved with the stealth and expertise earned from years of staying alive. He knocked the brave to the ground, their fierce struggle began, each man knew what failure dealt. Flint's urgency to find the woman drove him to end the battle in swift measure.

Shoving off the body, Flint crouched, ready for another attack. Meeting only silence he came to his full height. Where she hid herself captured his thoughts. Damn, he didn't even know her name.

"Darlin', it's Flint. Where are you?"

Nothing!

Angrier than he imagined possible, he fought for self-control, he needed clear thoughts to find her. The others would be here soon.

Backing up from the body now lying in the hiding place where he'd left the woman, Flint started a methodical search of the area. Without the moon he'd never have seen the broken branch. Moving cautiously to it, her tracks were too clear. "The ravine?"

Shaking his head, there were too many arguments against her going that way. She obviously knew these mountains better than most trackers. The answer proved so obvious. Of course!

She set out her own false trail. Thinking it through, Flint felt sure she would have doubled back to this area knowing he'd return.

"Come on missy, where are you?"

Like a hunter fretting out his prey Flint's eyes and senses began an intense scan of the area, stopping abruptly on the outcrop of boulders directly over the dead brave. The strangest feeling came over him as if he could read her thoughts.

Holding to his conviction, Flint began climbing his way up the rock face. Standing above the rocks he instantly found the small form wedged between two large boulders. She lay, unmoving.

Flint managed to force himself to move past the foreboding he felt. She hadn't answered him, and he'd been directly below her. His steps quickened, until he stood only a foot from her.

"Oh Darlin'..." Bending over her his hands gently eased her head back in his direction. The heat passing into his hand was shocking.

"Hey missy, it's Flint."

Watching the battle she waged to open her swollen lids drew a furious groan from deep inside him. When she tried to sit up, she said, "The brave...careful."

"All taken care of Darlin'. Now, let's see if I can salvage you as quickly." Picking her up Flint faced a terrible feeling of urgency to get her the help she needed.

He thought of taking her back to the cave, but dismissed it knowing she needed more attention than he could give her there. The Fort appeared to be the only answer.

Unfortunately those braves would know it as well. He didn't hold much faith they'd quit, especially once they found their dead friend.

Flint still held the remainder of the night on his side. As he moved away with her, he realized just how small she honestly was, making him wonder if she possessed enough strength to fight the fever. "Hang on little lady. I'm not fit to be around when I get riled and you giving up would certainly do that."

He carried her for hours before the delirious ramblings started. Flint talked to calm her fevered outburst. "Damn, if I don't wish you were really with me. I need your knowledge of these mountains right now. I bet you would know a place we could make a safe camp."

But the girl went too deep in the fever to hear him. Flint needed to rely on his own expertise, something he never had cause to doubt before today. "That was before you came along." She certainly turned into an unexpected worry. Strange, it didn't upset him. No, she'd given him a lot to think on since this morning.

He checked the moon's position. It would have to wait, right now he needed to find a place where they could hold up.

His image came clearly before her...then sadly faded. So many times she came so close to reaching him only to be pulled back into the hot darkness. Hell? Had she gone there? What did she do that was so terrible to deserve such a sentence?

She'd been a good girl, honest. So she did deliberately loose John Holly in the woods. He deserved it trying to force her to accept his sloppy kisses! She did feel sorry that the rescue team had been called out, she could have told them where he was, would have if they hadn't found him before dark. At least he never bothered her again.

Laughing, she knew he'd been too embarrassed to tell on her. Not even Grandpa guessed the truth.

Grandpa Longman. The tears cooled her cheeks. She missed him so much. The cabin wasn't the same since he died. Jolene felt the loneliness now. Not even her beloved mountains could fill that hollow feeling.

"...the stranger...love." Silly fortune-teller and her nonsense, "Never should have gone. I'd be home in bed, not out in the storm."

Again her cry filled the confines of the pine bough hut he'd erected. He lifted her back into his arms and tried to ease some hot broth past her dry lips. For two days the fever refused to let up. He'd only left her side that first morning to insure the Cree were gone. He'd followed them nearly two miles before feeling confident they didn't pick up their trail. The false tracks he set sent them off cussing and fighting among themselves.

"Take a little more, that's it." He needed to move her today. He dreaded what it might do to her, but he feared not reaching the fort and getting her proper attention. The girl touched something in Flint and each moment he stayed in her company drove her invasion deeper.

All her strange ramblings failed to tell him where she belonged...except for the mountains. She grew up here. Everything she spoke of centered around these mountains. He learned about her grandfather. Once she'd thought him to be the beloved man, William Longman. When she started crying, Flint sensed the man's death must be the cause. It didn't appear to be anyone else in her life. He wondered how long she'd been alone up here. The thought brought back that strange anger concerning her that he still couldn't put into words.

Breaking camp, Flint decided the people at the fort would know where she belonged. Besides, he still held obligations to the wagon train that should be at the fort by now. McKean would be in a fine state over Flint's absence. Flint hoped McKean's business would be concluded so they could move out right away. He wasn't looking forward to the last half of this job, not with the additions to McKean's group.

Looking over at her he muttered, "Trouble, that's what I'll have, nothing but trouble."

CHAPTER 3
Shock Treatment

Flint waited in the hall for the Captain's wife to shut the bedroom door. His impatience made him approach the lady, "Mrs. Pratt, how is she?"

"Fine Mr. Flint, now that the fever finally broke. I just knew my herb tonic would do the trick."

"It seems to have worked, Mrs. Pratt. Is she alright, I mean…" The Captain's wife took his arm, leading him toward the stairs.

"Can't tell yet, she hasn't really woken up, but I'm sure the girl will be fit in no time." She smiled up at the big man. "After what you said you both went through, it is no wonder the fever took such a hold. That nasty bump on her head didn't help none."

Flint should be relieved. She was better and being cared for by the Captain's wife, so why couldn't he let it go. Explaining her to the Captain and McKean hadn't been easy. At least he possessed a surname for her. He felt lucky no one asked him for more. The fact no one ever heard of the Longmans is what really worried Flint. How did a girl like her stay hidden? Neighbors might be miles apart, but not a one went unnoticed.

"A shame."

"What is, Mrs. Pratt?"

"Such pretty hair, too bad you needed to cut it."

Flint stiffened over the skeptical tone from the woman, "Didn't have time to do otherwise." Why was he lying for the girl? He should have left well enough alone.

He never found the chance to ask her why it was as short as a man's. Nor about her outrageous attire—pants, out on the trail he didn't have time to question what covered her limbs. Honesty told him he liked the way they hugged her soft curves letting him see exactly how they moved.

But Flint didn't like the way Mrs. Pratt and the other ladies clucked like nervous hens about it, and he'd jumped right in like some wet nosed kid defending his sister. Honesty made him admit to himself that his feelings towards her were a far cry from brotherly affection!

Besides, he didn't think Miss Longman would appreciate his help, probably let into him for it. That is if he were still here when she found out. Flint said his goodbyes to the Captain's wife and hoped the girl would have her wits about her enough to let his excuse stand.

Would he be here? McKean didn't show up at the fort until a day after Flint came in with the girl. Mrs. Pratt did for the girl what he couldn't out on the trial. The herbs sweated the sickness from her last night. "Damn it, she's not my concern!"

"Oh there you are Flint. Come in, McKean and I were just discussing the auction tomorrow."

He just bet they were. Facing these two pompous men took all of Flint's control. The white wig now donning McKean's head matched that of the Captain. Seeing his boss in gentleman's attire didn't change the lack of respect Flint held for the man. He never regretted a scouting job before taking on this one with McKean. Maybe if the man himself were stronger, more aware of the dangers out here in the wilderness. Maybe then Flint might hold the man in some esteem. It was a useless thought and after everything else Flint should have expected the worse. Now he would be witness to this so-called auction, a proceeding he truly wanted to avoid.

"Yes Flint, we've wasted enough time. No offense Captain, your hospitality is flawless."

"None taken sir, I can understand your need for haste. Tis' a bold undertaking to head out for unsettled territory, especially with all the savage uprisings of late. I have it on good authority it is the French that are behind their current revolt."

"Did you see anything besides those Cree, Flint?"

"No." They were enough, but Flint kept his thoughts to himself. Leaning back against the door he wondered just how much these two colonial gentlemen really wanted to know about what might be happening outside the guarded walls of this fort.

Captain Pratt built a nice little settlement here, still well within civilization borders.

Now McKean, he was a greedy man. Taking a grant of enormous size, he'd tacked on promises of land, riches and a gentleman's future to lure the men out of their feathered beds. Flint only saw one major flaw. McKean's land sat in French territory, the fact it was wilderness in its rawest state never entered the man's vocabulary. Flint wondered what excuse McKean would use, when the first soul got massacred by any number of Indian tribes now claiming the same land.

"...yes, that will be fine. We'll hold the auction tonight then. It will give the couples a night to get acquainted, so to speak."

The two men's laughter filled the room. Flint's leave went unnoticed. Another of McKean's promises to his land holders...brides, indentured brides to the highest bidders, right off the English boats to fill the beds of his unsuspecting settlers. He'd thought of everything to keep them happy and recoup his cost in the bargain!

Scowling, Flint needed some fresh air. He held no liking for the practice, selling one's self to another, it was barbaric. That these women were doing it for the security denied them in England sickened him further. What kind of safe life would they find out here?

None of them retained the slightest inkling of the hardships ahead. What troubled Flint further is that he would be one to lead them into it. Taking the men there might be bad enough. Seeing women slaughtered and carried off to worse fates sent his rankles up.

"Hey, Flint!"

"Brewster," returning the hail from the wagons.

"Heard you brought in another wench."

Flint stopped in mid-stride and turned back to the man. In deadly calm his question came. "What do you mean, Brewster?"

Unaware of the volatile anger coming to life before him, the man answered. "Heard McKean paid the Captain a good sum to include her. Seems they lost more coming over then they figured on and she being without family and such, the Captain agreed real quick like, not wanting another mouth to feed this winter..."

Flint's thunderous blue eyes shot up to the window of her room, before they nailed the man to silence. "Like hell!"

Releasing her tight hold on the quilt, Jolene couldn't stop staring in disbelief at the closed door. "How dare that woman!"

Wrapping her arms around herself in a protective hold, her violent denial didn't change the scathing reprimand she'd just suffered from Mrs. Pratt. "Harlot! My god, what's going on around here?"

Nothing made any sense to Jolene since waking this morning. Though her head finally seemed clear, the rest of the world existed in chaos. She refused to see the antiquated things all around her. "Now this!"

The woman's hateful remarks wouldn't leave her.

"Tch, and here I treated you like a daughter. Had my way you'd be wearing the mark befitting your scandalous behavior. And he such a nice man, owning up like he did, wouldn't be surprised if he lied. You probably bewitched him."

Jolene's hand raised to her hair over the condemning glare the older woman staked on her.

"Probably didn't cut it a'tall, probably some good folks marked you for your sinful way and he being a good man and all, he felt sorry for you."

"Listen up harlot, you'd best be grateful he's making you a decent woman. No telling how another would take your scandalous ways."

Under the force shaking her, Jolene didn't know if it came from shock or anger. "I've no desire to stick around here and find out which one of us is crazier!"

She tried to dismiss the woman, "She's probably senile, heavens she sounds as if she just stepped off the Mayflower." All Jolene cared about was leaving and going home. She wanted nothing to do with these people that Flint brought her to. "It's probably some religious or back to nature cult I haven't heard about. Well, they can keep it."

Jolene couldn't allow the painful thoughts concerning Flint to get any stronger. Because he failed to come and see her, she could only believe he'd left.

"That witch probably sent him packing." But it hurt that he didn't say goodbye. After everything he'd done for her since those fanatic Indians were chasing them, it just didn't fit the feelings she held for him.

Her stumbling steps maddened her, and she grabbed at the folds of material wrapping about her legs. Jolene refused to look any closer at the homespun cloth held within her fingers. She wanted her jeans back and wished she'd found the nerve to ask Mrs. Pratt for them after her bath. As Jolene searched the small room she hissed out in anger, "She probably burned them or something."

It didn't matter, Jolene would be leaving. Her mind set on going, she blamed the remaining stiffness from the fever for the hesitancy of her hand on the rawhide string door latch. She refused to acknowledge the uneasy feeling concerning this odd room, Mrs. Pratt and the remembered dangers on the trail. Nothing would interfere with her present goal. "Everything will be fine once I'm home."

Thoughts of saying goodbye and thanking the Pratts brought a sour taste to her tongue. To leave without doing so would be rude. The pride seeded in her, from a strict upbringing, wouldn't allow her anger to rule.

Squaring her shoulders, her pert chin rose a little higher as Jolene prepared for what she expected once she joined the voices downstairs.

"It is a shame that the Longman wench hadn't been included with the others at the auction. Would have given you a nice profit, even just recovering from that fever, she's healthier than the other women in the sale."

"Now McKean, you heard Mrs. Pratt. Once my dear wife gets that righteous gleam in her eyes, well I for one won't stand in her way."

"You are right Captain. Maybe we should feel sorry for Flint. Did you see how taken back the man looked over your wife's decree?" McKean slapped his leg before releasing a deep laugh. "Never thought I'd see that man at a loss, trapped himself dead on he did. But can't say as I blame him, she's a right pretty thing."

Neither man noticed the woman in the shadows. Nor could they see the stark terror seizing her pale face as she fled down the hall. When she heard Mrs. Pratt coming, Jolene ran back upstairs to her room. Leaning against the closed door Jolene gazed about the room searching for a way out.

She pushed away from the door, stopped and turned back sticking the wooden peg into the latch. She almost cried out with her desperate need to escape when the window pane wouldn't budge. Ready to pitch the first thing at hand through the window, her panic stilled over the thick bent nail protruding above the glass pane, turning it up the window moved. Jolene spoke to relieve the fear taking hold of her, "What could be worse than selling me?"

This place and its occupants were more horrible than she'd first imagined. The realization sent her running back to the bed. She stared at the object she went back for with a sick feeling. Her hand closed about the sheathed handle of Flint's large hunting knife. The wide sash about her waist was the only place she found to tuck it into. For the climb down the roof she needed both hands.

Crawling out through the window, Jolene cursed the cumbersome costume the woman forced her to wear. "Gratitude my foot. I'd rather face those Indians again."

She should have picked up the warnings from the woman's deadly stares at Jolene; the way she shook her head when Jolene refused to wear the ridiculous contraption across her breasts. "Probably the first of the witch's torture." It was archaic pushing her breast flat in until they bulged up over the bodice. When Jolene pulled the thing off, Mrs. Pratt turned crimson. How much of her ample cleavage showed above the stiff upright lace wasn't any better, but at least she could breathe.

Feeling the cold night air nipping at her thigh Jolene thanked the outdated wool socks and petticoats for their warmth. The full skirt layers rose up to her waist as she edged down over the eaves.

Flint thought he finally lost his sanity and gave into the haunting image following him. "Trouble, she's been nothing but."

He wasn't sure if his need to strangle her elegant little neck caused this vision to appear. All he admitted is that she suddenly became a sight he'd never tire of seeing. "Damn that woman doesn't know the meaning of convention!"

And at the moment Flint was enjoying her rebellious display too much to tell her. Even in a dress she seemed determined to flaunt those shapely legs...and cute backside. He should be concerned over why he just caught the girl crawling out of the Captain's house and down his roof, but Flint suspected why she wanted to escape. The truth started licking the flames of his anger for what he felt drove her to take such on outlandish escape route.

Hanging by her fingertips Jolene said a silent prayer the ground below would come quick and gentle when she let go. The contact never came.

Instant awareness stilled the frightened scream as the familiar hold moved up her legs, easing her down against the solid frame. "Flint."

Hands on his wide shoulders, she looked down into his raised unrelenting blue eyes. Captured, she didn't question that he still held her waist to his chest, no, his heat proved too overpowering to flee and Jolene's unbidden response came out in a slow sultry smile.

"I thought you'd left."

There was no mistake in the hurt brightening those evening shaded eyes of hers. *If only he could.*

"Going somewhere, Miss Longman?"

Awareness over the sudden hardness beneath her hold on his shoulders made her stiffen. Was he angry...with her? Realizing where she still remained and what he must think, Jolene struggled for release as her returning panic took over.

"Flint, let me down."

"You never told me your name."

She stopped her fidgeting and looked into his eyes, "It's Jolene." God, his eyes could make her forget everything. "Flint...I must leave here."

The lack of conviction in her voice felt like a splash of cold water, already they could have discovered her flight. "Please, these people are insane." He would help her, yes she knew he would. "Flint, I heard those men talking, it was awful," her voice lowered. "Flint, they actually spoke of selling...women...me! And that woman, my God, she acted as if I'd committed a mortal sin or something! Flint I can't stay here!"

Flint realized she didn't know, at least not all of it.

The intense rippling beneath her fingers made them rise off him in alarm. She searched his guarded features and sucked in her breath over the potent anger she glimpsed. "Flint?"

He never moved or blinked, making her breath come in short strained gasps.

"Where do you think you can run to...Jolene?"

Why did she feel scared of him? His arms tightened about her, everything told Jolene he'd stop the flight she sought. Didn't he understand? "Home, to my cabin, please Flint...let me down." The muscles in his fierce jaw jumped beneath her gaze. "I don't understand Flint. What is wrong?"

No, he'd known she wouldn't understand. He'd been enraged over what McKean and Captain Pratt planned for her. Storming into that room all logic disappeared over that infernal instinct she unknowingly stirred up inside him to protect her right from the first! His own arguments to turn and leave were flung aside over the powerful rage that took hold of him. Killing those two open-mouthed men wasn't beyond him at that moment.

"The Longman girl isn't to be included!"

McKean was the first to come out of his shock.

"Now Flint, I know you feel responsible, saving her and all, but she's already in debt to the Captain and besides she's alone, without anyone to come for her. It is the perfect solution."

She didn't need anyone, at least not the way they wanted!

"You're wrong...she isn't alone."

When Mrs. Pratt's controlled question came up behind him, Flint never released his stance against the men.

"I don't mean to intrude Mr. Flint, but maybe you should explain."

"Now Mary..." The Captain's awareness of the potently dangerous man before them, made the man move cautiously towards his wife.

All the decisions over what Flint needed to do ended in light of the Captain's wife. The Captain and McKean weren't going to change their minds. Snuffing the life from the bastards wouldn't help the unaware girl upstairs.

"Your wife is right Captain, I should explain...Miss Longman and I were alone for sometime..."

The reddening color on the older woman's face ended Flint's explanation. He wondered all night over the explanation he might have given if Mrs. Pratt hadn't taken it out of his hands.

Bringing Jolene down before him, he never released his hold about her waist.

Staring down into those violet orbs Flint knew her struggles to break his hold were useless, her objections wouldn't matter. The innocence driving into him couldn't be denied, neither could he dismiss what he needed to do to keep it safe from McKean's fate and what lived out there on her mountain.

That he would be taking her into the midst of the very threat he wanted to keep her from would be unavoidable. Thoughts of leaving her here in Mrs. Pratt's care were quickly dismissed. The girl wouldn't stay put. For all her courage, he feared what would happen to her. Jolene didn't seem aware of the dangers around her. Was it her gentle soul that put the blinders up before her lovely eyes? Flint sensed something very different about her. Flint hadn't been able to shake the feeling that she appeared lost.

No, he couldn't let her go.

Jolene's nervous denial came out in broken breaths against his betrayal. "I can still make it to the woods...Please Flint!"

"I'd have to stop you."

"Why? Why are you doing this to me? I won't be sold off! This is absurd!"

She'd forgotten how fast he could move when his arm locked her own beneath them and pulled her roughly up against his bold frame. The fact he actually used that capable strength against her made Jolene's panic rise to the surface in anger. "Release me, you..." None of her heated words rendered any effect, except to drive his chilling scowl against her.

"You've been running wild in those mountains too long, Miss Longman."

"Wild, Mr. Flint! You have no idea how untamed I can become!"

The slow serious smile he answered her fury with made Jolene's struggles increase. "You're probably right. I hold no doubts I'll soon find out."

Lifting her in his arms he effectively trapped all the flaying attacks she strove to release against him. Flint thought for a moment about trying to explain, but her next words cut as deep as the nails she wanted to scratch him with.

"I hate you. You're worse than them and I thought you were decent and kind! God, I'll get you for this, I swear I will!"

"No doubt." Telling himself her words came from anger didn't soften the blow. And again, he commanded himself not to give in to the feelings she called to the surface.

To do so would destroy the spirited woman. His own act against her would be enough for her to suffer.

CHAPTER 4
Revelations

Mad and hurt over the disappointment she harbored against Flint, Jolene wasn't prepared for his next assault. Setting her on her feet he prevented her flight in the unrelenting hold he maintained on her arms, pinning them to her waist as he pulled her back against him.

"I suggest you get on with it Captain."

Jolene's incredulous gaze went from the two men present, which made her lean back against Flint as if he'd protect her from their vile threat, to the condemning Mrs. Pratt. All the woman's horrible words came back at Jolene in a breathless rush. The implications she'd failed to understand before crystallized over the man's response to Flint's command.

"Young lady, I suggest you accept this marriage in the gratitude that it deserves."

"Her name Captain, is Miss Jolene Longman."

Flint's strong authoritative voice didn't diminish the words Jolene remembered from Mrs. Pratt. *Marriage...Harlot!* Jolene felt her knees go weak.

He didn't need to see her face to know of the shock settling in against him. When she tried to break his hold, he turned her to face him. Overly bright the unspoken question held in her gaze leveled against his own determined one.

Shaking her head in denial, "Why?"

If they'd been alone he could have told her the reasons, but..."Don't fight me on this Jolene...I don't want you hurt."

Blanching before him, she felt as if he'd struck her making her weave dangerously. When his hand reached out to steady her she backed away.

Staring at him and the others that shifted nervously behind them she found no compassion or understanding. Her pride reared against their condemnation and the searing pain one special man just inflicted. Facing Flint defeated her. His eyes were so hard set against her he turned into a stranger where a friend once stood.

What they all expected revolted her gentle senses. "Lies." Hissing out at him she wanted to get away. Without thinking her hand drew out the only weapon left to insure her flight.

"Jolene..."

His warning was lost to the trapped and frightened girl now before him.

"I won't be sold in any form!"

He caught Mrs. Pratt's movement towards Jolene before she did and took the advantage.

"Now really child, you are being very unreasonable."

Jolene knew her mistake before she turned the knife to ward off the woman's advance.

With shocking accuracy Fling reached her, the pressure he applied to her wrist took away the last of her fight. The tears that fell down her flushed cheeks were all he could stand. "Now Captain!"

Flint never released her from the locking embrace against his chest. The Captain began reading the marriage rites.

When the question came to her the tightening of his hold at her back brought forth Jolene's weakened reply. Denying that awesome anger glaring down at her went beyond Jolene's strength. "I do."

Flint's vow came in bold command across the dampness on her cheeks.

Jolene's lips parted over the eminent kiss. Her eyes closed against the unexpected gentle taking, as if he were sorry for what he'd done and told her in the only way he could.

Numb to all except the man still holding her hand, Jolene stiffened when Mrs. Pratt came forward. When the lady actually hugged her Jolene grew stunned by the woman's whispered words. "Never believed a word my dear. Don't be too hard on him it really was the only way to stop my husband and Mr. McKean's decision about the auction. He's a good man, you'll be fine in his care."

Her mouth clamped down over the wink and smile the lady gave her as she pulled back. More confused than before Jolene wondered if she were going insane. She could feel Flint's gaze on her and stubbornly refused to be drawn by it. She had a good idea of exactly what Flint implied to these people. His lie simmered her anger into a slow boil. Cautiously, Jolene studied the room. He may have forced this, but she didn't have to stay around.

When his large hand took hold of her shoulder she wondered if somehow he read her thoughts. Leaving wasn't going to be easy. She'd just have to be patient, choose just the right time. He couldn't stand guard over her forever.

The storm surrounding her intensified as other unwanted feelings began over his burning touch. Unable to handle the rocking emotions Jolene needed to put some distance between them.

The time he'd spent with her in the wilderness honed Flint's instincts where Jolene was concerned. "Captain I think my wife has had enough excitement for the evening, after her illness."

Flint tried to hide his mirth at the instant flash of anger she failed to disguise. He'd get no rest this night. Flint needed to remind himself of exactly how capable a woman his wife could be. That alluring pixie image cloaked her formidable abilities, along with her elusive beauty. All soft and seductive, her shimmering coppery wisps of hair framed her cameo features and large lavender eyes. She could appear wild like the young boy he'd believed her to be at first or a seductress, who could wield her innocence like a frail child driving a man wild with that primitive desire to cuddle and protect the treasure he found. If she ever suspected his thoughts her infernal control wouldn't keep the torrent behind those thunderous eyes in check.

"If you both follow me to the study, we will sign the papers."

The Captain started talking to Flint about the groups taking their leave in the morning, drawing him to the desk. Only half listening she used the situation to disengage his restraining hold practically daring him to stop her. It proved a foolish display on her part when he effectively blocked the only way out of the room.

Flint's gaze followed her casual movements about the Captain's room, not fooled for an instant over the convincing interest she pretended to have over his books. God, he'd have to be careful not to let his guard down, she'd be gone in an instant if he did.

"Ah, Mrs. Flint, you're a lover of books?"

Never turning from the volumes, Jolene answered. "Yes, I am. You have an impressive collection of first editions, Captain."

"Please my dear, take some with you, it is a long journey."

Why did the Captain's offer surprise her in such a stunning manner? "Oh, but I couldn't, these are precious."

"I insist. In fact I have duplicates of many already crated. The last shipment was a double order. Such a shame too, it will take nearly a year for the right order to arrive from England. The ship sailed last week, what with winter fast approaching, I doubt we will see her back in the harbor until spring."

Flint forced himself not to go to her, but he felt the muscles in his back tense in readiness over the shaking that caused her to hold the bookcase for control.

When she unconsciously sought his help with that remembered look, Flint knew something went drastically wrong. "Jolene?"

Her head gave a quick shake, "Yes, well, I best sign the papers. I am feeling a bit tired."

The Captain smiled at her and took control, "Please, sit here in my chair." He turned the document about to face her, "Now, you sign down here, beneath your husband's name."

She only half listened to the instructions. Her eyes were fastened upon the parchment, noting every scripted detail.

...before me in the presence of Captain Pratt, married by the power of King George the First, entrusted upon his servant in the year of our lord 1713, the 16th day of August...

Closing her eyes she took a deep breath telling herself it couldn't be real. But everything that happened since she came awake after the mudslide forced every detail forward in shocking race to reality.

Dipping the quill in the inkwell he placed it in her fingers. "All looks in order, now this line here, yes...that's it."

As if she'd lost all will over her hands they did as he asked. Above her fluid signature rested the large bold script of Allen Flint.

When his fingers closed over hers the quill fell away, all her strength suddenly vanished. Jolene held the most terrible conviction that she couldn't run far enough to escape...time!

"Come Jolene." Flint sensed the weakness that fell upon her with a striking force. Holding her hands in his he stilled their silent shaking. "What's wrong, Jolene?"

He'd never seen her like this.

"It's 1713?"

Her frightened question sent a chill up his neck. "Yes."

"Please Flint, take me away from here?"

The desperation he heard and saw in her overrode all the warnings. She wouldn't run. He sensed something beyond her ability to fight just captured the woman clutching his arm.

They walked in silence through the torch lit compound. Flint didn't miss the way she pulled her eyes away from the things they passed. It seemed as if she couldn't bear to acknowledge them.

Mud kinked log huts, open cooking fires, wagons and carts of all sizes. Muskets, horses and people...early Americana, no...colonial America. Her hand went down to touch the homespun cloth of the borrowed dress. The woman all wore similar grays or browns, all the earthy colors that nature's dyes afforded. A few of the men wore buckskins like Flints', but most bore the knee-length pants above stockings and boots, with long coats of wide cuffs, ribbed fronts that held the influence of British militia in detail. *Year of our lord 1713...King George...*

How did this happen to her? The images of the Indians came back in frightening detail. "They were real."

Her words stiffened his already tight muscles. Softly he asked, "Who were...Darlin'?" The endearment came naturally to Flint as if understanding she needed the gentle meaning.

"They weren't Cherokee?"

He wanted to help sort out her confusion. Keeping to their easy pace he supplied the information she sought. "No, they were Cree and further north than they are known to frequent."

"And these people?"

"They are Mr. McKean's settlers."

Stopping, Jolene turned and looked up at him.

Flint made himself remain still and fought down the urge to hold her. Whatever caused this in Jolene, it appeared too important not to let it run its course. Again, his feelings over how lost she first appeared to him, came back tenfold.

"And you, Allen Flint, who are you to these people?"

"I am their guide to the Louisiana Territory."

"A scout?" Her eyes ran over the competent man. "Yes, of course you are."

"Jolene, can you tell me what's wrong?"

Jolene gave him a smirk, not all her anger with him disappeared. No, not even believing she actually woke up in another time could dismiss what he'd done against her. "Like you told me Mr. Flint? I recall my question was never answered."

Before he could recover from her attack, she began walking away. His long strides easily reclaimed his position at her side.

"I'm relieved to see you are recovering...Mrs. Flint." His emphasis on her new title made those small shoulders come back.

"Are you always so sure of yourself, Mr. Flint?"

Stepping in front of her, Jolene had little choice but to stop. With more tenacity than she felt she looked straight into his agitated gaze.

"My answer is simple Jolene."

Is it? But Jolene never voiced the question that mirrored her own confusion.

"I too had no intention of seeing you sold off like a piece of meat!"

Her eyes grew larger over his shouted explanation.

When he grabbed her arm and led her away from the gathering onlookers Jolene kept her smile hidden. It would be a grave mistake to give in to her humor. Knowing her nerves were breaking and the slightest nudge would send them flying.

He dragged her along beside him, "You are an infuriating woman, Mrs. Flint."

"And you sir should have thought about that before trapping me in such an outrageous situation."

Pulling her behind a large tree Flint pinned her to it. "Would you have preferred the alternative? The women you see out there came over here from England with the sole purpose of finding a husband and God help them, a better life than the slums they left."

His words were the finishing touches on what Jolene could no longer escape.

Seeing her stricken look, Flint couldn't ignore his own feelings for her any longer. Pulling her into his chest, when she wrapped her arms about his back, his hand cupped the cap of silken hair. "Ah, Jolene, I didn't mean to harm you. There just wasn't any other way to stop them." Maybe he shouldn't take this any further, but Flint needed to try and make her understand. The anger between them couldn't remain. "Neither could I allow you to run off to your mountain. The danger they hold in their shadows is something you'd never survive. Those Cree shouldn't have been up this far. The Captain was right when he mentioned the French were instigating the tribes against the settlements. I fear what's coming, knowing you would be alone out there...damn it Jolene, I couldn't let you go!"

The fevered release he gave into opened her own. Unable to stop herself, Jolene buried her sobs into his broad chest. Just having him hold her, stroking her shaking body, gave her more comfort than she could ever remember. She cried for so many lost things. If it were only her desperation that made her seek what he offered, she didn't care. All Jolene understood was that Allen Flint somehow entered her life, and she didn't want to lose him.

CHAPTER 5
Stubborn Ox

"The big brown fella there, he would be the mean one. You stay clear of his back legs." Mr. Simon clucked and scratched his head at Jolene's skeptical gaze upon the oxen.

"Go on Mr. Simon, tell me what else I should know about them."

"No offense Mrs. Flint, but does your husband know that you have never worked a team before?"

Husband? It gave her such a queer feeling to hear Flint paired with her. "My husband has no time to be bothered with this. Please go on."

Both their gazes went to the man galloping past. "No, I reckon he's got his hands full with all the others."

"Exactly, Mr. Simon."

Trying to keep her attention on Mr. Simon's instructions about the four oxen proved difficult when her eyes kept straying to Flint.

"Now, to turn them...Mrs. Flint, unless you feel like chasing these here oxen over the mountain, you'd best listen."

Dully caught, Jolene's blush softened the man's stern features.

"I'm sorry Mr. Simon."

"Humph. To stop them, you hit them here."

"Doesn't that hurt them?"

"They be rightly named madam."

This, the whole morning that started at least three hours before the sun started to rise, came close to her expectations over sliding down the falls.

Sighing, Jolene's mind drifted again to last night.

The memory held her warmly against the cool morning air. Flint not only dominated her attention, he became the focus of her unsettling existence. The same kind of funny feeling she remembered from her first day in school, started last night after her tears calmed. How could she have ever doubted his kindness, when it enfolded her at every turn?

When they'd finally come to where Flint set up camp, far from the others. Jolene's stomach tightened into knots. Everything she now accepted about really being here seemed incidental in comparison to the man now claiming to be her husband.

Wife? Was she? She knew what she expected last night. But now she wasn't sure. When he lay down beside her she turned so stiff with uncertainty that when he put his arm around her she knew he must have felt her tremble. She held her breath, eyes clamped shut, and she waited. Seconds became minutes before she realized he didn't do anything more than hold her. She was breathing so hard her breasts were pressing in agonizing awareness against his chest. When he moved she froze, but the trailing finger down her cheek held no threat, nor did the warm pressure of his lips on her brow. "Go to sleep Jolene, we have a long day tomorrow."

She waited for more from him. It took some time to realize that he had no intention of exerting his marriage rights. Finally, relaxing, she slipped cozily into the easy embrace he let her find.

The big brown eyes and grinding mouth came back into focus. She needed to get a hold of herself.

"Well, that's the lot Mrs. Flint. This here's the finest team and wagon about these parts, should do ye well for your journey."

"Thank you Mr. Simon, I am sure they will."

When the man left her, her guarded gaze went back to the four large animals now in her care. "I hope he's right."

The arm sneaking about her waist made her giggle in surprise. "Who Mrs. Flint?"

Resting her head back against his shoulder. "Why Mr. Simon, of course." Flint made it easy to want him near her.

"Are you ready?"

Was she? "Yes." She told herself she must do this.

"I'll try and stop by after we get away."

"I will be fine."

"I know you will."

His confidence in her wasn't reciprocated by Jolene. If he knew how inadequate she felt among these people...no, she couldn't find the courage to tell him about herself. Maybe she never would, heck, she barely believed where she stood.

"Jolene?"

"I'm sorry." She must stop losing her concentration.

Flint tilted her chin up, "It's still there."

"What?"

"That fear that came over you last night."

She tried to drop her gaze away, afraid he already saw too much.

"Uh, uh, you can't run from it, can you?"

When she didn't answer, he did. "No, I thought not. When you're ready to tell me, I'll be here...I'm not going anywhere, my Darlin'"

His kiss came quick, but when he would have pulled back Jolene's hands gripped his collar and stilled his retreat, surprising them both when she deepened the caress. Flint needed no more encouragement as he pulled her fully against him, parting her willing lips, driving to possess and Jolene moved into the flame, headless of the devouring blaze.

Pulling back before he lost all control, Flint rested his forehead to hers, taking in her heated breath as it mingled with his own. Cupping her flushed face between his large hands he brought her heavy lidded eyes up to look into his own. "Madam, I've never claimed title to the dubious label of gentleman, and after the torture I inflicted on myself last night and now, only sampling the heaven I denied us, I've no intention of changing my ways."

Dropping his lips to her petaled seduction, Flint growled over what kept him from finishing this. "Tonight, Jolene, if you can find it in your heart, I want you to be my wife in all ways."

Shaken by her own rapid desire for this man, she didn't recover fast enough to give him the answer he sought. To his retreating figure on the horse racing away from her, "Oh yes, Allen Flint, I too want to be your wife."

"You're as stubborn as old man Grant's mule. Move it you red devil!" Tapping the big eyed ox on his backside, Jolene blew up at her wet bangs.

"His hide's too thick for a tap, if'n you don't mind some advice ma'am."

Spinning about at the voice she didn't realize she held the staff like a weapon until the skinny boy stumbled backwards. She let go of the stick and let it fall to the ground. "I'm so sorry."

The scrawny shoulders shrugged, "you got to smack it."

Taken back by the boy's scruffy appearance she caught her mistake in the tightening of his thin lips. "What?"

"The ox, hit him like you mean it."

"Oh." They stared at each other a moment longer before she realized the cart in front of her had a good ten feet lead. "Oh stars!" Stomping her foot she turned, determined to make the animals move.

She did hit him harder, nothing happened. Jolene just couldn't make herself use any more force against a "dumb animal."

"Ain't dumb, just ornery. Here, let me try."

Before she could object the lad took the staff and with a few well-placed and obviously knowledgeable moves he got the team to plod out into the line of carts.

"Thank you, I guess I need more practice."

"Watch me for a while, it gets easier after the first day."

So even the boy knew she was a novice. Deciding not to fight her good fortune, Jolene fell in step beside the boy. He looked about nine or ten. His bare feet made her bite her lip to stop the questions that rose. It became clear that the boy's lot was not a favorable one. She told herself it wasn't her affair. She truly possessed enough problems of her own without jumping into someone else's.

"My name is Jolene."

"They call me David, Mrs. Flint."

Alright, so casual wasn't a part of their ways, she needed to remember. "Are your folks near us on the train?"

"No missus."

Jolene's stab at conversation failed miserably, David's only enthusiasm came over the oxen, something he appeared to know well enough. His lessons with her went slow, but she eventually lost her fear of the staff and animals. By mid-morning Jolene held a fair grasp of the oxen's particularities.

Flint rode by many times during the day. On first seeing the boy Jolene met his questioning gaze. She shrugged in answer to the unspoken question, not wanting to say anything in front of David.

Unfortunately, the demand for Flint became so great during the day that Jolene only caught glimpses of him. It seemed Jolene wasn't the only one unfamiliar with the animals. She learned from David that a lot of the men didn't purchase their wagons or cart until reaching Captain Pratt's fort. Ninety percent of the women were the ones Flint spoke of from England and Jolene could see for herself they didn't come off any farms.

Most of the dresses they wore were inadequate for the harsh trail through the woods. The thick brush and cut away stubs left by the men at the front of the line, were cruel to feet and cloth. More than once she saw strips of satin or a piece of ruffle hanging from the sharp, freshly cut stumps. She couldn't see many of the women, except those close to her wagon, but if they looked as haggard as these she pitied them. She understood the anguish in Flint's words to her last night. The sullen faces of her neighbors said they didn't find what they expected.

Jolene said a silent thank you to the amazing Mrs. Pratt. The woman surprised her again this morning by showing up at their wagon. Not only did she have the books in tow, but a trunk full of clothes!

All of Jolene's arguments were brushed aside. "They were my daughters, no need now to keep them." The pain she witnessed in the lady's admission forbade Jolene from voicing any questions. Hugging the lady, Jolene thanked her for the clothes and then for Flint. The woman left in a state of happy sniffles.

There hadn't been time to satisfy her curiosity over what might be in the trunk. In fact, Jolene couldn't imagine what kind of things might be in the wagon. It and the oxen came with Mr. Simon this morning. She decided Flint must have scrambled to obtain them and the supplies. Smiling, it made her feel better knowing that he really didn't plan what happened between them. His confession to her made it all the more special.

Looking around at the high mountain ridges surrounding them, he was right, she didn't know of the dangers. She still found it hard to imagine the threats that common sense said were there. The thoughts came slowly to her today over something Flint said about the French and the Indian trouble. If what she believed would be coming, the chill it brought would only be the beginning. The French and Indian War remained one of the bloodiest in the Colonial history.

She would have to tell Flint. How he'd take her knowledge is what scared her. He wasn't the type to not want answers. He'd already told her that this morning. But would he believe her?

Her worry over his reaction took away from the pleasure she found on the trail. Unlike the other women Jolene excelled out here. The differences she faced didn't change the fact that this was her home. The Appalachians were a part of her life. Hiking and camping with her grandfather since she could remember, every summer she traveled the Appalachian Trail. As she grew older she went out with hiking groups. She felt a little smug that she actually felt familiar with the terrain they moved through. Of course, she almost laughed out when it came to her that she'd actually been following the same wilderness trail these last years. "It is harder with the oxen."

CHAPTER 6
Gifts

The woman's scream filled the air, stiffening, Jolene spun about. "David, take the team."

Running towards the shouts, pass the curious, Jolene broke through the gathering group to find a woman sprawled out on the ground in obvious pain.

"What happened?" Jolene directed her question to the man kneeling beside the woman.

"Don't know, she just screamed and fell."

Kneeling down Jolene didn't wait to be asked, the signs coming over the stricken woman told her what was wrong. Pulling up the dusty purple satin and torn slip, she stripped away the dark stockings. As she suspected the sick swelling about the two puncture holes was spreading up the woman's leg.

Taking the hose and a stick Jolene applied a tourniquet. "Hold this and don't let up the pressure until I tell you." Looking about her, "You, give me your knife."

The man passed it over, no one said a word, Jolene decided they were either in shock or awe over her actions making her wonder if she should be doing this. But not helping the woman went beyond self-preservation.

"What kind of snake was it?" The man finally asked what his faced showed.

Holding the knife above the wound she met his worried gaze. "A copperhead."

His eyes went to the spreading poison before returning to Jolene. "She won't make it, will she?"

"I don't know that, but I have to try."

His nod sent Jolene to do what she needed to. "Hold her down!"

The men moved in to do as she said. Cutting a deep cross over each puncture the woman's scream vibrated in her ears. When she began to squeeze, trying to extract as much poison as possible, it grew horrible to listen to. "I've got out all I can this way. Carry her to the wagon. I will need hot water for a poultice." When they didn't move fast enough, her voice rose. "Hurry! I need to go find what I need. Keep her covered, she's going to start feeling the poison. Release the tourniquet for a steady count of thirty, then retighten it for a hundred. Repeat the process until I return."

The man nodded and started directing the others and ordered the gaping women to fetch water and get the fires going.

Rushing off into the woods Jolene started her search for the black snake root.

"Slow down and think. Remember what Grandpa always told you, in the soft shade of the cottonwood the bitter root grows." Lifting up her skirts Jolene began running over the obstacles to reach the tree. Dropping to her knees, her frantic digging finally released the roots. Folding the plant up in her skirt she headed back.

Never stopping Jolene raced through the assembling camp until she found the wagon. Taking what she needed from the plant she mixed the steaming water in until the thick paste formed, she realized the root should be dried, and she prayed it would still work.

They laid the woman over by the cart. "Hold her, its hot."

Jolene could already see the effects of the poison on the woman. She applied the paste to the red, swollen leg. "Don't let her shake it off. As it cools and dries it draws out the poison through the skin. If we get enough out before it reaches her heart she will have a chance. I need to go find some more before I lose the light."

Jolene hoped they listened, she didn't have time to linger doubting anyone else would be able to find the plant. She wanted to make a tincture to give the lady, it wouldn't hurt to try both.

The woods never bothered Jolene, not even when the shadows grew long. So the ill feelings coming to her now as she reentered their depths made her skittish of every noise. Everything seemed different here, and she felt her heart pounding wildly by the time she rushed from the dark forest.

The camp fires looked inviting, but she didn't like the uneasiness that seemed to hang on.

Trying to save the woman named Charlotte, soon stole all of Jolene's thoughts.

Struggling to rise, Jolene felt the ache in her bones. "She will need to rest and stay off the leg for a few days."

"I'll fix her up a place on the cart."

Jolene nodded her agreement. "Make sure she gets down some of Mrs. Clive's broth."

"Mrs. Flint?"

Turning back, she faced the man. "Yes, Mr. Strokes?"

"Thank you, she wouldn't have made it without what you did for her."

"You just take care of her."

"I will, you know we just married the other night, but Charlotte, well she is a good woman."

"Mr. Strokes?"

"Yes Ma'am."

"Tell her that, when she wakes up. You will be surprised how much it will help her recover."

His sheepish grin spread over his face. "I'll do that, right enough."

Her steps were slow through the meandering camp. Strange how one incident like this could bring people together. Jolene returned the friendly waves given as she passed. Sighing, new people brought new friends.

Walking into her own camp she was surprised to see the stew pot over the fire.

"How is she?"

Turning to face Flint, he stepped out from beside the wagon.

"I think she will make it."

"The stews ready."

She took the bowl he offered. "Did you do all this? It is wonderful."

"Tired?"

"Hmm, thank you."

"I'd like to accept, but I found it like this when I came in."

"Then who could...David? Do you think he did this?"

"Could have. Who does he belong to? I don't recall seeing him before this."

"He never said."

The rabbit stew soon took precedence.

Sitting back down beside Flint, after cleaning up the dishes, he pulled her into the nook of his shoulder.

"Did your grandfather teach you all that doctoring?"

"How'd you know about him?"

"Your fever, you spoke of him a lot during the worst of it."

"He was like you in many ways, Flint."

"He teach you about the mountains too?"

"Grandpa taught me the basics as he called it. Like snake bites and he taught me how to see things, like the ants beneath the moving leaves or the bats that give away secrets."

"The cave."

"Hmm, yes. I told you it would be hard to find."

"They showed me." His fingers played with her hair, "And the mountain?"

"Those near my home I learned from him. It was my own giant playground."

"Where was home?"

She didn't miss his use of the past tense, but now wasn't the time. "At the end or beginning of the Appalachians, depending on your outlook. In what I believe is called the Virginia colony.

"You were some distance from there that morning."

The warnings sounded, "I often hiked the mountains."

"You weren't hiking, you were hurt. Why do you shy from telling me what put you there?"

His hand dropped to her shoulder, and she felt him tense beside her. "I'm not, I...well I often went far from the cabin. I've even been through this area."

She could have bitten her tongue for saying that.

"Were you alone?"

His anger vibrated beneath his concern. Sitting up she tried to make light of his question. "No, of course not." She needed to stop the way this was heading. "Flint, why do you make camp away from the others?"

He knew exactly what she was up to. He almost told her the most important reason, but... "I can hear things better out and away from the camp noise."

What could she say? "More coffee?"

"No." He started enjoying her nervous ways when cornered. What he didn't like was her refusal to tell him what stood behind the very clear fear her answers held.

"How is it Jolene, you didn't know those braves were Cree? It seems someone as familiar as you are with these mountains would be aware of what lurks in them."

She'd known he wouldn't let it go. "Don't be silly Flint, of course I am aware."

He didn't let her make it to her feet. His hold about her waist brought her back, and he pinned her beneath him. "You are a terrible liar Mrs. Flint. Maybe you could have fooled me if I didn't know how capable you are...except in this particular area. I'd go so far as to say you are totally ignorant on the subject of two legged predators."

Her quickening breath didn't go unnoticed making it hard to stick to the subject he wanted answers for. "What's wrong Jolene, run out of excuses?"

"Don't Flint, let me up." She pushed on his chest. He didn't even flinch at her insistence, making her give up the struggle.

"How did you end up so far from your home and why does the telling scare you?"

The gentle stroke of his hand down her cheek grew distracting.

"I want to know and I will."

The half shake of denial she started to give him quickly ended. She faced his determined stance, knowing she already lost the battle. "I don't fear it any longer. I'm only scared now of what you will think if I tell you."

"That's all the more reason to get it out in the open Jolene. I don't want things to stand between us."

She believed him, but would he feel the same if she gave him what he wanted? Did she have a choice? "All right, I will tell you...I was in a flash flood, the downpour must have caused it."

"Why were you out in a storm?"

His thumb absently moved over her shoulder, making it hard to concentrate on her words. "I had an accident."

He knew perfectly well what his caresses were doing to her, Flint hoped she didn't. He wanted to get this out of her, and he'd use whatever method necessary to accomplish his goal. "What kind of accident?"

A warm tingling started low in her stomach, making her shift under him. "My...car hit a fallen tree."

No, she didn't say cart. "Did you hurt your head then?"

Nodding she closed her eyes when his finger began to trace the top of her bodice over her breasts. Feeling him touch her, made her feel so excited, so expectant...

"Tell me what happened...Darlin.'"

He released the bodice's draw string, giving him more freedom to touch her.

"I, I left the car to go to the cabin, but the slide pulled me away." Oh God, his lips were doing wild things to her. "Please Flint, I can't think."

"What happened next Jolene?"

"I don't know...I woke up and I couldn't find the cabin or the road, nothing. I kept walking down, knowing I should find the highway or a house...everything looked different, but the same. I got all confused."

"Lost?"

"I guess so. I didn't know for sure, my head hurt so much."

"Why did you try and hail the Cree?"

Jolene's words were as broken as her concentration. "I...help me, take me to civilization, I didn't know they were real, not savages like they used to be, it's not like that anymore. Oh Flint, that feels so...good...I can't...couldn't think, the Indians I know are not dangerous, they wouldn't think of shooting arrows at someone."

It was all he could do to go on, past the warnings. Using his thumb and forefinger Flint played with the harden nipple of the breast, cupped in his hand. She squirmed beneath him. "When were you born, Jolene?"

"July 19th."

"What year?" She went still and Flint knew his question delivered an impact.

Strange how he knew he just found his answer by the way she stared up at him in panicked understanding. Trapping her hands down beside her head,

"What is the date of your accident?" Her head shook violently against his question.

"What year were you born Jolene?"

He used his weight to defeat her struggles to rise. His thigh locked her against the ground. "The date wasn't 1713, was it, Jolene?"

Her body grew still as their gazes locked. Her silent plea for him to stop didn't penetrate. "Tell me Jolene. Tell me why you are afraid?"

"Flint..."

"Say it!"

"I can't!"

"Born? When Jolene?"

"1984...oh Flint please, I don't know how it happened. I just woke up here. I didn't know the dangers they posed because I never faced it before I met you." She tried to free herself from his hold, but he'd have nothing to do with letting her end this.

"Tell me what a car is?"

"What?"

"A car, tell me what it is? Come on Jolene, tell me."

His insistence made the words pour out of her to explain. He pounded questions at her until she grew breathless and exhausted.

"Please Flint, I can't answer anymore. I will, I promise, but not now I am so tired."

He didn't doubt her. His deliberate firing of questions had their affect. They also gave him all the proof he needed. No one could make up lies that fast. In each answer, he'd pick one word and throw another question at her, trying to trip her up. Car led to oil, oil to fuels, fuels to transportation, ships, trains, planes, cities... She held the knowledge to throw out the words without thought of the context.

"How did it happen Jolene?" Sitting back he lifted her with him.

"You believe me!" Her hands gripped his shoulders. "Don't you?"

"Oh Darlin' I always have believed in you. What's hard to grasp is just how it happened."

"I don't know..."

"Hush, I know, I guess I'm just going through what you did last night. It was last night that you faced it?"

"Yes, the books." Her laughter held little humor. "The Captain's books would be worth a large fortune in my time. He's not exactly the type to give one away."

"Hardly."

"But it was the marriage certificate. The words about King and Lord, then the date, it just brought it all into focus."

He held her close to ward off the uneasy feelings Jolene's answer just delivered. "You mustn't tell anyone else about this, Jolene."

Tilting her head back to see him, she frowned over the dark strain in his eyes. "I trust no one but you Allen." She placed a light kiss across his tight lips. "Thank you for believing me."

How could he deny what she just showed him? "Always Darlin.'"

At that moment Jolene understood that a power beyond her brought her to this man, but as she leaned forward to feel Allen, Jolene realized it would only be their magic that held them together, now.

There wasn't any gentle asking in his embrace. Jolene surrendered to a claiming kiss and the door to ecstasy opened under his masterful caress. Could a woman glory in being conquered? The sweet warmth of his fevered lips said she could.

She groaned when his powerful hands stilled her racing excitement, holding her head back as his fingers delved into the silken threads of her hair. His lips burned a trail of fire over her closed lids to the tiny lobes of her ears, licking and nipping the sensitive flesh about her ears. Jolene moved against him pressing forward to sate the fire he ignited.

"Allen, I want you to love me."

The name no other called him sounded husky and warm from the sensual woman awakening in his possession. "Yes Darlin', I too want my wife."

Like dawn's brilliant haze she smiled and beckoned his ardent caresses. That surging emotion, one Flint never felt before, suddenly came forth with a power so strong it rocked him. Protect and cherish, the emotions ran rampant through his blood, but there was also a dominate desire to rule the passion he released in her. Wild and untamed she turned into a living fire in his embrace, one that he feared would never be vanquished.

"I want to see you Jolene. I want to touch your ivory curves, make you want me with the same wildness I carry for desiring you."

Her response moved around him like a sensual and alluring dance. She rose before him with that seductive air she always exhibited to him. For all her boldness he sensed the tantalizing innocence racing just beneath the heat of her passion.

They needed only the cloaked moonlight for their zealous fires held their own light. She reveled in the way this man looked at her. His eyes burned in hunger over her, like a feather they touched her skin and like a flame they left their brand. He made her feel beautiful and wanted; Jolene always wondered what it would feel like to have a man desire you. To have it actually happen set free a tide of explosive excitement moving through her body, one that kept gaining strength beneath his intense blue eyes.

The dress fell soundlessly about her ankles, only the chemise remained to cover her straining full breasts. Flints' ardent gaze fell upon the dark, sultry evidence of those desirable nipples. So proud, they appeared above the firm heavy globes.

A moment of sanity stayed the overwhelming urge to rip away the thin barrier keeping her sweet flesh from him.

Rising to his full height Flint gathered her in his arms. No distance was far enough from the camp for the feelings coursing through him.

Jolene's soft laughter flamed the skin at his neck. "You move like a cougar, my husband."

Capturing her lips he smothered her sultry purrs as he took them deep into the woods. Setting her down on a blanket of thick grass his patience deserted him.

Jolene's eyes feasted on the magnificent male form standing in all his naked glory before her. Every firm muscled contour gloried in being bathed by the moonlight. "You are beautiful, Allen."

She caught the rise of his eyebrow, but refused to be chastised by his manly pride. *Proud, oh my yes, he possessed that and so much more.* Slipping the material from her shoulders she watched to see his reaction and what his gaze did to her flesh left her gasping for breath. Her hands moved in deliberate slowness over her breasts, lifting them in wanton display before moving down the smooth plane of her stomach. He only hesitated a second before going lower to touch the dark curls covering her pussy. She smiled when he sucked in his breath as her fingers parted the dark sultry folds to expose the most sensitive part of her sex to him. "Touch me Allen."

His hand reached out and caught her about the waist bringing her slowly to him until their bodies touched and blended together. "Perfection in ivory satin, my Darlin'. You shimmer beneath the stars."

Jolene's low moan of awareness grew husky as she moved up his frame, grinding her heightened sex over the solid force of his arousal. She'd never touched a man like this before, and she could feel her instant sexual response. Hot and fluid, she just turned on as if by magic. "Oh Allen, I want to feel you."

If he thought of arguing, the words were drowned by the touch of her hands closing around his thick shaft. It throbbed and jumped as if fighting the taming caress she instinctively caught him in. Up and then down the full length as if exploring every inch of his erection. Flint's hands took hold of her butt kneading the cheeks soft tightness as he pulled her closer, trapping him against the satin flesh of her stomach to still her hands now touching him in growing boldness. "Ahh, my wild, sweet Darlin'."

His arms wrapped around her small frame holding her as if they could become one. He felt her lips burning a forbidden path down his chest...and moving lower still. Flint's hands massaged her back but didn't stop what he felt coming from her. And when the soft warmth of her lips closed over him Flint's head went back in male ecstasy. No woman ever touched him so intimately; the truth of her lips sucking in sweet earnest on his sex drove deep, touching his male pride. His strong fingers dug into her hair, she was his...his woman, and he would now be her man!

The woods filled with the cry of his male awareness.

Jolene's purr of satisfaction flowed with those of the man now taking possession of her. She turned into pure fluid in his hold as he gently lifted her and placed her on the forest floor. And when his thighs pushed hers apart, she tried to guide his pulsing head to the entrance of her vaginal heat. But his hands moved hers away and pressed them into the grass over her head. Jolene's passion ruled as she arched up, touching the heart of her sexual passion to the throbbing length of his shaft. "Take me Allen. I need to feel you inside me!"

Her head fell back as he moved the head of his powerful sex over her heat, spreading and mixing their passion's fluids. His gentle probe drew her anguished cry for more. And when she felt him take hold of her hips guiding her in position to receive him she tried to rise up, but Allen controlled her. Jolene's arguments died beneath the erotic touch of his fingers moving over the core of her sensual heat. She excelled in his proud rule; if he meant to conquer she would be the willing captive of his masterful ways. He drove her unmercifully until her body cried for what he promised.

"Jolene?"

"Oh yes, Allen..."

His lips came again, and his tongue battled for the undeniable dominance he now exerted. "Yes, my wife."

"Now Allen! Love me Allen, please."

"With my life Darlin.'"

Her hands framed his face and their heated gazes locked in understanding. Flint moved to claim the woman that somehow became the focus of his life. His hands held her ready for him, and he drove into her, past the seal that wanted to keep him out...and his kiss silenced the cry from the girl that just became his...woman!

CHAPTER 7
Discoveries

"He's back."

She didn't have to look to know Flint spoke of David. The boy stood at the edge of their camp. Meeting her husband's harsh gaze, she knew what stirred behind it.

"Jolene..."

"I know Allen. I'll try, I promise."

Sighing, Flint relented. "Go on, take him his breakfast." Flint watched her rush over to the fire and scoop up a man size portion of porridge for the boy, he swore under his breath. "She's going to take in every stray in camp."

Flint shaded his gaze from the boy in order not to send him running. Flint thought Jolene's meals put some meat on the boy. He wasn't as weak as his wife thought. The boy possessed the wits to escape all of Flint's inquiries. Oh, the lad knew Flint was on to him and yes, Flint felt a flicker of admiration for the boy's ability to elude him so far. Not once did Flint manage to track him back to where he went each night. Flint hadn't found any answers from any of the other people in camp. No one seemed to claim the boy or know who did. What it told Flint left him uneasy.

Only Jolene could get close to the boy and then only at a distance. And when Flint came into camp, he wouldn't even come within the circle of the fire light. Flint knew he only had himself to blame for the boy's skittish behavior, but his need to find an answer for the lad ruled all other feelings.

When Jolene came back to him, "I need to get them moving."

"Will you be going out to scout ahead this morning?"

Her sly question didn't fool him. Pulling her to him, his arm locked her halfhearted attempt at false modesty closer. Laying his forehead to her, she always smelled so fresh, like a field of summer flowers. "You know I am. I should be back by night fall."

Wrapping her arms about his neck, "Not should Allen Flint, just be here."

Their gazes locked in silent understanding that tightened Flint's throat.

"Such a demanding wife you've become."

She rained kisses over his fierce jaw. "Demanding, loving and damn cautious, and you better be the same my husband."

Holding her chin still Flint captured those dewy lips in a hungry kiss. He broke the contact before it got any harder. "No man could stay away from you any longer than a day...Darlin.'"

Before he could pull away her hand gripped his arm, "Flint... do be careful."

Kissing her brow, "I always am."

Jolene fought the urge to call him back. Had it only been three weeks? Hugging herself to hold his warmth about her, "Such wonderful weeks my dear sweet husband."

Hearing the noise directly behind her pulled Jolene out of her dreamy thoughts, turning and facing the boy she unconsciously ruffled his blonde hair. "All done, David?"

"Umm, I'll get the team hitched?"

"Sure, go on."

Every morning he asked her the same question. As if by her acceptance he would once again be welcomed for the day. Her shielded gaze followed the boy as she packed up the wagon. He was looking healthier. Jolene made sure he ate, even past Flint's scowl.

Oh, my dear husband, she couldn't help but smile thinking about Flint. He wasn't upset over the food, she knew that from the start. In fact, she knew perfectly well where Flint's concerns laid over the boy. That he refused to admit he cared about David was something she accepted from him. She'd learned a lot about the man now a part of her life these last weeks.

The most unsettling knowledge for Jolene came from his total disdain for his involvement in with McKean's venture. Flint told her how he loved scouting and the mountains. What he didn't like was bringing innocents, as he called them, to the wilderness. He worried over what they would face out here, and she couldn't blame him, not when she knew what could happen better than anyone.

He talked about it with her because he wanted her to know the dangers. She decided she needed to help Flint after a group of British militia came across their path last week. The massacre horrors the soldiers told McKean and Flint about were only the beginning of the horrors they would all soon face. Flint spoke of his anger over McKean's grant being in "French claimed territory of Louisiana", a fury that intensified after what she told him would come. He insisted they would depart from the settlers once he got them to McKean's land. He told her he owned land up in Massachusetts that they could build a home on. They couldn't reach it before winter, but they could stay in Richmond at his brother's until spring.

The thought she might be disrupting time or something by telling Flint what history held did cross her mind, but letting Flint go out there without the knowledge she possessed proved impossible. Sometimes letting him go, like this morning, nearly killed Jolene. History held a dark side and the man she instinctively knew she would spend her life with was captured in one the bloodiest eras for the colonies.

Jolene wondered if Flint spoke of settling down only because of her presence in his life. Could he give up the wandering? The answers were something she still needed to find. For now, their lives were a part of McKean's group and Jolene decided that Flint's goals would be her own. She held no desire to be in the midst of the troubles the French and British conflicts would bring to the colonies, any more than Flint wanted her to be. Jolene realized Flint could not make this plodding group move any faster than the oxen allowed and the going proved painstakingly slow.

She almost envied Flint his time out on the mountains scouting. Once, she tried broaching the subject of accompanying him, the flat no she received didn't leave room for weaseling. It was a shame. Mrs. Pratt, the dear, packed her jeans in the trunk.

Jolene even found her car keys wrapped in a handkerchief with a note from Mrs. Pratt. The lady believed them to be a valuable heirloom the likes she never saw before, but sure that Jolene would want to keep them safe.

Having proof of where she came from drove her to race through the wagon train that day and find Flint. She nearly dragged him away from Mr. McKean and into the woods. To be sure no one but Flint would see the keys she made him follow her deep into the forest until he finally scooped her up in his arms and twirled her around and around.

"I think we are far enough away from camp now Darlin.'" His desire darkened his gaze as his lips lowered to take her in a swirling kiss of passionate bliss.

Jolene decided the keys could wait as her eager fingers closed around the swollen shaft of Flint's lustful erection beneath the leather pants. He helped her free the wanting part of him that jumped to reach her, but Jolene desired their time together to last a bit more and she moved slowly from his arms, letting his fingers linger over the damp evidence of her own readiness to take in his magnificent length.

She loved the way he would watch her undress for him. The way his gaze would travel over her flesh, taking on this hungry look that she knew only she could sate. Her own need to feel him buried deep within her made her go to him in all her naked glory. She moved up his fine steeled body, kissing her way to his waiting lips and when they took her, and he lifted her to him, she wrapped her legs around his waist and in slow madness took in the full, throbbing length of his sex.

Buried to hilt, she pressed harder until her clit rubbed against him, causing her vagina to contract and dance about his shaft, before slowly drawing back over the powerful length. It became an agonizing, sensual dance of rapture that they both gloried in, until Flint could take no more and his large capable hands took possession of her, and he drove himself deep within her slick heated folds. Faster, harder until they were both grasping and holding each other tighter and when that pinnacle of glorious release exploded between them she swore they both floated above the ground in erotic ecstasy.

Later, as Flint's calming caresses gentled her quivering body, Jolene remembered the keys. She jumped up and straddled his muscled waist to reach her dress and the wrapped treasure. She wasn't beyond teasing him as she moved her heated sex over his sated member, smiling when it pulsed and started to seek her touch once again. Keeping it trapped beneath her she wanted to show Flint her treasure before they made love beneath the night sky once again.

The night would be one she would pull out and remember many times as one of her happiest moments. Flint's gaze teared with her own over the real evidence she shared with him. She realized he never doubted her claim of time travel, but it made her feel better that he actually held her car keys. When he spoke his thoughts her heart swelled with love for this marvelous man.

"...You must miss your world, Jolene."

She waited for his gaze to meet her own. Smiling she placed the palms of her hands on each of his cheeks, making sure he saw exactly how she felt. "I do Allen, it would be hard not to. But this...the force, it brought me to you Allen, so you see my dear husband, I will be where ever you are. If it were to whisk us up and drop us in the future as long as we are together, I don't care." And with each word she kissed his face until her lips covered his and his hands refused to let her escape his thorough kiss. Before she realized it Jolene was beneath him, and she opened to take his possessive rod into her velvet folds...

Looking at David when he called out that all was ready, Jolene brought her thoughts back to the present. But not before she smiled, the keys were safely tucked away behind a panel in the trunk. She stilled missed wearing her jeans. How she longed for their freedom over the dresses. Jolene wanted to scoff at how the dresses and skirts made her feel feminine, but remembering how Flint's glance would roam over her and give his silent compliments for the care she took with her appearance, it was worth all the trouble. Not a day lapsed that the trail's dust wasn't washed away. Even the boy was clean. Jolene's insistence met with stubborn refusal from David, but the threat of being tossed out of her days, sent the boy to the basin to scrub off the layers of grime.

Personal hygiene didn't seem to be a priority with these people. Flint laughed at her dismay. His own personal cleanliness was excellent. He teased her and said it was only so the Indians couldn't smell him a mile away. When she'd honestly believed him he'd teased her unmercifully, saying she was gullible. Some things about her new life she just needed to accept. Only in her house, even if it existed outside, she would be a stickler for cleanliness, and she realized there were more than a couple jokes floating around the camp about it.

Mr. Stokes didn't complain. Her daily changing of Charlotte's bandages and clothing may have earned smothered grumbles, but for his wife's recovery he'd have scrubbed the oxen if Jolene insisted. Thinking on the Stokes brought a smile over her. They were only married a day longer than she and Flint, it made it nice to know others fell in love as fast.

Sadly, Jolene faced the truth that it wasn't always the way. More than a few domestic problems surfaced since the start. For all his faults McKean proved to be a good mediator and so far he'd managed to patch up most of the fighting couples.

Jolene still harbored ill feelings against McKean, though he did try to make amends. His frequent invitations to take dinner at his camp weren't all for business with Flint. Begrudgingly, she'd accepted his apology. She felt his peace offerings were more for Flint's benefit than hers. Her husband's protective stance concerning her became well known and McKean needed Flint. She hoped the man wasn't lying about the letters of acceptance from the French government for the grant. If it turned out not to be as McKean swore Jolene feared what Flint's reaction might be. He felt so responsible for these people.

"They are moving out, Mrs. Flint."

Jolene managed to place the iron pot on the hook under the wagon. "That's the last David, move that beast out."

The boy's laughter was something rare, like the blue bird she spotted yesterday. She hoped David would become more at ease around her.

Remembering her promise to Flint made her teeth set. He was right, they needed to know where David went at night. She saw how Flint tried to follow David and his anger over being duped. But she also understood her husband better than he realized and Flint's ire came from concern over the boy's safety. David's own leeriness of Flint kept the distance between the two of them. She'd seen David's eyes follow her husband. How the boy tried to imitate Flint's long strides. Jolene watched the admiration given from afar on both counts.

But the farther they went from settled areas, the more dangerous it became. If David truly slept out in the woods, alone, it couldn't go on. Jolene already decided there wasn't anyone to claim David, be it by choice or otherwise. She did worry over Flint's reaction if his fears proved true. His conviction against these people settling in the wilderness went double for women and children. The fact the boy latched on to them wasn't setting right with Flint.

The morning went by with Jolene lost in her troubled thoughts over David and Flint. She couldn't seem to shake her worry over Flint being out there scouting. But she usually worried when he left camp, she figured all her worry rested more on the problem David posed than Flint's safety.

By mid-afternoon, Jolene put off dealing with David as long as she could. She couldn't decide on a good way to approach the boy.

David must have sensed Jolene's dark mood for he'd been more quiet than usual. So, when he abruptly spoke up it startled her.

"Why are you afraid for him today?"

She couldn't hide from those piercing blue eyes. They could be as intense as Flint's at times, but a lighter shade, like the sky above them, where as Flint's were deep and dark like the blue in a raven's wing when the sun caught it just right.

"I guess it is because we're getting deeper into the unsettled territory."

"I heard what those British soldiers said about the raids on those settlers. It won't happen here."

She didn't remember seeing him around McKean's camp. The guards the man always kept about his wagon told her David must have been in the woods behind them. "Why are you so sure David?"

"Because he wouldn't let them get you."

She wondered what Flint would say if he could hear his little defender. David could be so young in some ways. His quiet brooding made it hard to remember how young he must be. "You're right David, Flint would never let anyone hurt us." *Go on Jolene, say it.* "But Flint isn't always near. That is why he worries over you."

His quick look up at her showed how skeptical he felt.

"The woods are becoming more dangerous now."

David busied himself with the ox as she spoke.

"We need to be more cautious when we go out for wood and water. Do you remember what I told you?"

"A silence in the forest says there is danger."

"And?"

"And, be an owl, who looks all around, wise is the one that knows when to run."

"Very good. Now, I've got another one for you."

"More lessons?"

"Not lessons David, things that will keep you alive. These mountains can be your friend or your enemy."

"How so?"

"Well, say you are lost. Would you go up or down?"

"Up, so I could see where I am."

"That could work, if you have a landmark to go by. Take that peak over to our left."

"The big one? With the rock face?"

"Yes, that one. Now, all day it has been on our left, because we are traveling between the mountains, following their base. By tonight, we should be very close to that peak. If I got lost..."

"You would find that peak and then head to it."

"You are learning fast."

"What if it is dark?"

"Then I would climb a good size tree, wedge myself in between the limbs and stay put for the night."

"So nothing could get you."

"It is safer than the ground. Just like in camp, we keep the fires going to ward off animals. Do you sleep near the fire David?"

"Sure."

Jolene kept herself from looking down at his cautious stare. The lie vibrated in his voice.

"David, do you trust me?"

"Yes."

"Then you know I tell you the truth about the danger."

He nodded, but turned away from her gaze. She knew this wasn't working and decided on another tactic.

After a while Jolene gave an exaggerated sigh, for his benefit.

"What's wrong?"

"I'm just worried about a friend of mine."

"How so?"

"Well, it's a hard question. You see, my friend, who I care about very dearly, he's scared."

"Everybody gets scared."

"I know, but he won't let me help him and friends want to help each other. He is taking awful chances with his life, because he won't admit he needs help."

A long time passed before the boy said anything.

"Maybe he is afraid his friend will tell him to go away."

"Do you think a friend would turn his back on another friend?"

"Nooo...but, what if the friend is in trouble, in it real bad?"

"Most real bad things can be fixed. It is always easier when you have someone to help you." Jolene absently brushed the boy's bangs out of his eyes. "This friend only has to ask and his friend will be there for him."

For now, she'd done all she could and gave the boy a lot to think on. *One more day David, that's all I can give you.*

Unfortunately, Jolene's silent vow became lost to the shocking event of the evening.

CHAPTER 8
Troubling Decisions

Mr. Stokes had been the first to come to Jolene as David helped her set up camp in Flint's absence. The way the man avoided her direct gaze made her spine stiffen in warning. Her fingers dug into the bread dough when he finally spoke. His words made her fist close, the dough squeezed through her fingers.

"It's your husband...they found his horse."

Jolene swayed dangerously over the sick feeling that someone just stole her world. She ran her hands nervously down the front of her apron, "David, stay here."

"Yes ma'am."

Her legs felt weighted in dread, but quickly increased their steps. Flint would be fine, she couldn't believe otherwise. She pushed through the crowd of men. Jolene stopped at the assaulting sight. McKean held the reins of Flint's horse, but the broken arrow embedded in the saddle bag is what froze her in place.

"Now Mrs. Flint, he's a capable man..."

"What have you done to help him?"

She wanted to scream. The pictures assaulting her were horrible. Flint? Was he... No! Jolene wouldn't believe the looks in the stricken faces staring back at her. She brought her attention back to McKean, "I asked what's being done!"

"There is nothing to do, Mrs. Flint. It is almost dark and there isn't a man here that could do anything but loose himself out there."

Her head shook in disgusted disbelief at his fatal admission. Turning, she pushed back through the crowd before the crushing rage took hold of her and lashed out with all its fury.

"Mrs. Flint, now hold up, maybe we can get a group together in the morning."

Refusing to stop, "Morning could be too late."

"Now see here, Mrs. Flint."

Stopping cold, Jolene spun on the man, pinning him with a deathly cold glare. "Back off McKean, I've no time for your self-serving bullshit!"

"Madam!"

"No! It is wife! And that is my husband out there and by your own words there isn't a man among you willing to risk his precious neck. So stay out of my way."

Jolene didn't care about the ring of onlookers. She didn't have time to waste on McKean. The command he so liked to wield wasn't going to touch her.

"You are distraught, I understand, but these things happen Mrs. Flint."

"Not to Flint they don't!"

"I'm sure he'll be fine, he'll catch up with us."

She knew before he spoke his next declaration what would come. Practically growling at him, she stormed off.

The man jerking her to a halt earned him a Charlie-horse that broke his hold. "Don't ever touch me again!"

Rubbing his arm McKean straightened in caution. "You know these mountains as well as your husband!"

"Save it McKean. I'm not your scout, he is and without Flint you are as good as finished."

Walking up to him, Jolene nearly lost her bravado, knowing full well what the man wanted and what he might be capable of doing to serve his own needs. "The only tracking I'm doing is to find Flint and help him." To insure the man understood her, "I hold no responsibility to anyone, except my husband."

Before she could go, he pinned her. "You'd leave us here!"

Looking straight back at the man, "Exactly, just as you have seen clear to desert Flint."

The man paled. Not from her cold meaning, but from the angry nods of agreement from the people around her. When Jolene left this time they closed the circle, preventing him from following her.

Running into camp she called David. "Keep watch David. If McKean or any of his men come this way, call out."

David ran off to guard the path.

Jolene wasted no time in getting what she needed, including Flint's pistols and his hunting knife, before going into the bushes.

"Someone is coming!"

"It's Mr. Stokes, Mrs. Flint."

"Let him pass David. I'll be with you in a moment. David keep watch."

When Jolene stepped into the campfire light, the shock on the man's face made her groan.

"Mrs. Flint!"

"Mr. Stokes, I need speed and silence, something these clothes will give me." She knew exactly what he saw. A woman in men's pants, it didn't matter they were like nothing he'd seen on any man. With the laced ties of her buckskin shirt, she could imagine the sight she made.

"But..."

"I'm sorry if the pants trouble you, there is no choice. Why did you come?" While the man found his voice she slipped the powder horn and sack of supplies crisscross over her breasts. Taking one of the caps from Flint's things she put it on to cover her light hair.

From the ashes of the fire she rubbed the soot over her face and hands, hiding their ivory softness. The moon would be nearly three quarters full and would give her sufficient light to find his trail. It was also a light that could tell others of her whereabouts, unless she took precautions.

"I must be going, Mr. Stokes."

Clearing his throat, he regained his control. "We do understand Mrs. Flint, we all wanted you to know."

"Thank you. I am sorry...if..." No, there weren't any ifs, she would find him. "Tell McKean, to stay put, we will be back."

"But what if he won't listen?"

"If I were you, I'd take Charlotte and head back to Pratt's fort. That man will only get you in worse trouble. Just follow the trail we left behind us."

"You take care. I'll watch your things."

"And, David, please Mr. Stokes."

"The wife already insisted on it."

After she said goodbye to David and instructed him to stay with the Stokes, he escorted her to the men that found Flint's horse. Their information wasn't much, but at least it gave her a direction to begin her search.

McKean waited for her at the edge of camp. Jolene stopped about five feet from him, chin raised high over the way his eyes raked her body.

"I'm coming with you."

If this was some game of his to repair the damage he caused with the people, Jolene wasn't having any of it. A tiny spark of doubt made her scoffing remain silent. "I'm sorry Mr. McKean, but I go alone, one can hide easier than two." She prayed this would be the case with Flint.

The man's shoulders actually relaxed in relief. "I understand, I hope all goes well."

"Wait at least five days before leaving, we should return by then." She didn't tell him to go back, he wouldn't listen.

Free of the camp, the remembered teachings came back quickly to her as the night closed in. It wasn't long before she moved with an easy confidence.

The night sky shined beneath the clear sky. She came upon the clearing the men told her about. On her knees, her hands went over the torn up ground. The beat down grass leading away from the signs of struggle said he must still be alive. Forcing herself not to give in to the trembles, she started the tedious job of following Flint's captors.

Everything he'd told her came back in cold reality. It could be the Cree that caught him, or worse, the Iroquois. Jolene told Flint about the Iroquois active part in collaborating with the French. All the horror stories over what happened to captives shot through her mind. She struggled with her fears for Flint, she needed to keep all her senses on where and what she was doing. A lapse could mean wasted time in relocating the trail or being captured herself.

She was able to follow the trail up to where they crossed a wide creek bed. They were heading north, but she realized it could be a false trail to throw off any pursuers. "Damn it Flint, I can't lose you!" Giving up until daylight made her eyes smart *with* threatening tears. But Jolene refused to take the chance of missing their trail. The moon was low, she saw no other choice. "Find a tree."

She took her advice to David, wedging herself snugly in between a wide fork of a thick maple. The night sounded all around her. Leaning her head wearily back against the trunk she filled her mind with his virile image. She held to his strength, knowing it would help him to survive. "I will come to you, I promise Allen Flint."

The welts on his bare back stung furiously, as the sweat ran over them under the morning sun. Their vicious games with him went late into the night, but Flint held to only one thought to block out the pain each running step intensified... Jolene!

Damn, he knew his feelings were right, nothing would convince him she wouldn't try to follow. *So help me you greedy bastard, don't fail me now!* McKean was the only one he knew of that could stop what he feared from his wife.

A jerk on the leash about his neck cut off his wind until Flint caught up with the grinning brave. "Go on laugh, if my hands ever get free your filthy neck will be the first thing they take hold of!"

Giving the savage his own smirking tirade made the painted face scowl at him in answer. They enjoyed tormenting him, but they hated Flint for not giving in to their brutality.

Their pace increased, making Flint wonder where they needed to be. Of the ten Iroquois braves, the tall figure of the group appeared to be their chief.

They called him Awasos. Flint knew enough Algonquin to know it stood for bear, the man equaled his name. He stood tall for an Indian, just below Flint's six three, and they were equal in stature.

That close crop of hair that ran down the center of his shaved head ended in a thick mass of long dark hair, bound with an eagle feather. It lent a regal look to his barring. The man's dark eyes took just as thorough scrutiny of Flint. Unfortunately, Jolene and the danger she could be getting herself in because of him stole his concentration. It was a mistake that cost Flint to have his hands bound in back of him. The bear saw too much and caught Flint's obsession with the area they left behind. Grinding his teeth together to keep his rage under wraps, Flint knew it must be the reason for the man's absence from their racing group. The chief must have gone back to see if anyone followed.

Flint tasted his terror over the only one that would be capable of committing the feat. Everything he'd feared could happen to her, he may have caused to befall the woman he loved.

Ah, but he did love Jolene. He kept wondering if she knew how he felt. Why hadn't he told her?

CHAPTER 9
Tracks & Traps

The morning sped by before she finally found their trail again. Walking the creek bed, her instincts were right by going up stream. She found their tracks, and they were going north as she suspected.

By noon she found their deserted camp. Jolene stayed within the cover of trees and kept closing the circle until she picked up the direction they headed out that morning. The trail showed clear enough, almost too clear, making her internal alarms strike. Keeping parallel to their tracks she followed in cover. It was an aggravatingly slow process, but she couldn't help Flint by getting caught herself or killed.

The last thought stiffened her resolve to be careful.

It broke through her thoughts as only a slight sound, but one that froze all her movements. Parting the bushes she'd been crawling through, Jolene searched frantically for the reason of her heightened awareness. Arguing with herself, the doubts made her stay put.

After several minutes, nothing happened to confirm any danger. Still, plagued by the feeling someone might be near she started to edge herself along on her belly. *They are running and here I am crawling.*

But she didn't break her decision. She reminded herself that they were sticking to a deer trail, one she could follow easily enough at night. If they held to their habits and made camp tonight, she could possibly catch up with them by morning.

Sliding down the slope below the higher trail, the thick tree cover made the going easier. Coming across a large patch of blackberries, beneath a rocky overhang, she edged up between them. No one could see her picking the berries, but from her position she could see all the way down to the river at the bottom of the mountainside.

Her little feast gave back some of her spent energy. These last weeks of continual walking alongside the wagon restored the stamina that the classroom took away. Jolene felt in top condition.

One more and I'm out of here. But the plump berry never reached her expectant lips. There, below her, the slight movement cleared into the striking shape of a warrior.

Swallowing her gasp, she almost choked. The man moving in apt wariness through the brush honed Jolene's senses. This was no ordinary Indian. Iroquois for certain, there was no mistaking the scalp lock.

Sinking back into the shadows, God he looked so fierce!

Not even the Cree carried such a shocking impact on her. What she saw in the way he moved and held himself, scared the living tar right out of her!

Running was out. That he searched for her or someone that might be following them became all too obvious. When his face turned up toward the slope, she felt certain he must be looking directly at her and it was all she could do not to bolt in fear. Her breath finally released when he looked away and started on. She watched him scale a large group of boulders that hung out above the river bank.

What happened next surprised her as much as the man. The boulder he leaped upon gave way, sending the whole mass, including the Indian, down over the bank. Unthinking, Jolene rose from her cover, their gazes locked for an instant before he was pulled away.

Her chest heaved in indecision. She should run while she had the chance to get away. So why couldn't she make herself do it? Jolene started cursing him and then herself for her previous life, one that wouldn't let her leave a person in trouble, not even an enemy. All the warning didn't stop her legs from running down the mountain side.

At least she retained enough sanity to pull out one of the pistols and cock the hammer. Remembering how big he appeared she suddenly faced second thoughts, wondering if he could be hurt by anything.

Nearing the slide area she moved cautiously closer, only to see where and how he landed. Scanning the rubble her panic mounted when she didn't see him. Fearing he wasn't hurt at all and would jump out at her, she started to turn, but a splash in the water halted her retreat. When his hand broke the surface, groping for a hold Jolene didn't know what to do. Pulling on the rock they touched she saw the powerful fingers dig at it for a hold that pulled his face up to suck in the lifesaving air. When his fingers slipped so did his face. Again they came out repeating the process.

Oh, no, he's trapped! Without thinking she moved to find a sturdy branch. Finding one she dragged it out over the rocks to where she could see his shining form struggling beneath the surface. Placing the log where he could reach it, she braced it against the rubble, sliding a heavy stone over the free end to hold it in place. He found it, pulling himself up with both hands until his head broke the water.

Gasping and coughing for air he held on. His massive shoulders finally stopped vibrating as he regained his breath. She witnessed the bulging muscles tense before her eyes as he struggled to dislodge himself from the rocks.

Jolene could see that the boulder fell on top of him from the waist down, pinning his legs.

The heated words he sputtered couldn't be anything other than his frustrated curses. The harshness made her gaze jump back to his. Stepping back from the potent rage in the man, she felt his failure vibrate through her. She couldn't blame him for his anger.

The groan filling the air was her own, because she knew she couldn't leave him like this. Those fierce dark eyes of his, glared back at her in all their fury. Neither of them moved until his gaze left her and fell to the branch he held and the rock keeping it there.

Ignoring their shared anger over the situation, neither of them controlled, Jolene knew it was up to her to free him. She tried not to think of what might happened when he got free.

Jolene started searching for something to use against the boulder. She chanced a glance at him. He kept watching her with as much caution as dictated her own movements around him. No, he wasn't the type to hold to gratitude. She'd have to be ready for what she expected from him.

Finding another thick branch she hacked away the smaller limbs with her hunting knife. Satisfied, it took all her strength to get the pole over to the boulder. She needed to see where to place the end for leverage. Knowing he continued watching everything she did she refused to look at him. At the present time he wasn't a threat, but if she succeeded in freeing him, it would only be a question of who would move faster. Jolene counted on the water and maybe an injury, if the hidden grimace she caught once spoke true, of giving her enough time.

At the moment she'd done all she could except go into the water. It meant getting close to him, would he strike like a wounded animal against his rescuer? Jolene prayed those intelligent eyes held some common sense behind their dark intensity. Not caring she spoke out with the conviction and anger he presented. "So help me, you pull anything and I'll let you drown. It's bad enough you are keeping me from Flint!"

Setting the pistol and her gear on the boulder, out of his reach, she waded into the cold water. Taking a deep breath Jolene slid under, using the rocks she made her way to his position. The boulder was the one sticking out above the water. She could see his legs under it. The main weight rested on his thighs.

Resurfacing for air, she came up, nearly beside him. Shaken by his closeness and the way he stared at her, she made herself remember what she needed to be doing. She took another deep breath and went back under to clear away as many of the rocks and stones she could from the side of the boulder. She needed a brace, something flat.

Coming back for air she ignored him and searched the bank for the right stone. It took her several trips to place it in the sandy bottom beside the boulder.

Out of breath from her exertion Jolene sat for a few minutes before trying to place the log. Working with it in the water was the only option. Her anger with the stubborn pole's weightlessness in the water brought a half smile from the man's stern lips.

When the pole finally moved into the right position, Jolene knew she'd probably cry if it didn't work. The man couldn't last forever in the cold water, no matter how strong his thick arms wrapped around the log appeared to be.

She could just reach the protruding log. Getting a firm grip, she looked at him before trying to bring it down. She returned his silent nod and said her own prayer it would all work. The pole jammed under the boulder needed to lift it up without snapping, that is if she could find the power to bring it down. Practically hanging from it the log hardly budged. Pulling herself up onto the pole, she kicked up so her full weight came out of the water and onto the pole. Ever so slowly, the pole started to move down.

"Now!" She didn't need to shout out the order, the man already started fighting to get free. Pushing with all her might Jolene bore down on the log until her arms felt as if they'd snap in two. He used the log he held for leverage to pull himself out from under.

She knew when he'd succeeded, his victory cry shattered the air. Easing off the log, Jolene fell back to the bank and the boulder her pistols were on. Being in the water so long made her legs feel like lead when they touched land. The ordeal exhausted her.

Her hands and body were trembling when she reached for the gun. Turning to face him she held it out in warning to the man coming slowly up the bank. She wasn't sure if it was caution on his part that made him move so sluggishly or the accident. He didn't appear too concerned over the weapon she held on him and that worried her more. The little voice in her head told her he probably knew she couldn't kill him.

She felt her stomach tighten over the obvious that she'd just spent the last two hours trying to save his life!

CHAPTER 10
Ultimatums

Standing before her he seemed to come alive as he stretched to his full height and breath, flexing out the imprisoned arms and legs that had been inactive too long.

Awasos watched the woman's reaction to him and the life force returning to his body. The white scout had good cause for the bold concern he'd unconsciously displayed. But not for the reasons one would normally hold for a man's woman? He may have been trapped, but he'd seen and learned much concerning this man's woman.

The surprises went further than finding it was not a man he back tracked to destroy. He glimpsed on the woman's abilities before the fall that caused him to miss her presence. Awasos didn't find admiration in others easily and never in a squaw. The white scout showed to be impressive for an enemy. His woman proved to be no less so. That her skills saved his life weren't easy to forget.

His gaze went slowly down to the pistol, causing her to raise the barrel in determination towards his chest. Those violet eyes flickered blue in indecision, but he wasn't fool enough to ignore the reason behind her unusual presence. Mother bears with cubs couldn't be more dangerous.

The space between them became electrified to a volatile plane. Jolene's acute awareness of the man told her he wouldn't let her just walk away. Everything inside told her she would have to stop him to save the man she loved. "Don't make me regret saving you."

The stiffening at her words in the expansive bronze chest was unmistakable. "You understand me, good."

His acknowledgment was given in regretful resignation. She possessed the power to make a man forget his control and the warnings sounded loud in Awasos.

A slow anger started to take hold of Jolene over the obstacle he posed. She'd done what she needed to, but it hurt to know that by her own act she could have failed Flint. She could shoot him. A wound to those powerful legs would slow him down, but the thought repulsed her. Tying him up would be impossible, he'd never allow it.

The impasse played on her nerves. She needed to do something before he did. Her eyes darted to the low placement of the sun, adding to the truth of what she'd lost.

"Move back out, into the river."

His proud brow rose, the anger brightening his eyes helped her hold to her resolve. "The river or a bullet, the choice is yours. I may have saved you, but I refuse to allow you to stop me. Now move it!"

The moments before he finally moved were pure agony for Jolene. When the water reached his waist, he turned back to face her.

"Start swimming, I figure the pistol is good for three quarters of the distance to the other side, should you decide to turn back. Oh, I am also an expert shot."

She braced herself for what she felt would come from him.

The smile before his words is what made her knees grow weak.

"White scout's woman, we will meet again. Awasos is how they call me, run fast woman for I too am an expert...swimmer."

With that he plunged into the rushing current. True to his word the long, powerful strokes kept him on a straight course across the river's width.

Waiting only until he passed the middle, Jolene took off with his warning on her heels. The sick feeling in her stomach said he wouldn't be far behind. Outrunning him would be impossible. Frantically searching the terrain she made her decision.

Dropping down, out of sight, she went into the thick undergrowth and headed back to the river. She prayed he would believe her to try and follow the trail. Slipping back into the cold depths she pulled herself along the bank through the overhanging tree limbs. If he did find her, the river would be her only escape. Waiting until he gave up searching for her appeared to be the only way she could avoid the threat he posed. That he would still be out there, waiting, for her, never left her thoughts.

The moon rose high overhead before the bastard entered the night camp. Flint's furious gaze never left the man and his never faltered from his bound captive. The rawhide thongs cut deep into Flint's flesh as he strained to break free before the approaching man.

In full meaning Awasos's gaze drove into her man. His anger still high that she'd once again eluded his pursuit. But she'd come, of that Awasos felt as sure of her as the moon would soon fall away. He could feel his excitement over the prospect, one that matched the white's rage in knowing she remained out there. Awasos enjoyed the man's torment almost as much as he would in defeating his woman's attempt to save him.

Flint felt the man's knowledge of her in his gut. The wrenching inability to reach her tore Flint's rage out into the open. "You bastard, you harm her and nothing will stop me from killing you."

The savage showed no sign of the effect his wasted words had on him. Flint wanted to have his hands around the man's throat and his body rocked against the force keeping him from reaching the savage.

The cold words from the man standing before him left Flint immobile in scathing rage.

"She will come, regardless of the threat we pose. Unfortunately, her brave efforts won't save you...and in the end she will be defeated."

The veiled threat to Jolene raked across Flint's predatory male senses in brutal clarity. The savage's knowing smile cut deeper than any of their wounds. Flint suffered defeat when she'd fallen into a fever, but this...he felt helpless to help Jolene and it tore the soul from his heart.

Closing his mind to the disabling defeat, Flint couldn't let it rule. Nothing would stop Jolene, that bastard hadn't. No, Flint saw the savage's anger in failing to reach her. But they'd met, Flint's conviction over that fact struck too strong to be toss away. Awasos, the name burned in his throat. Flint didn't think Jolene would escape him again. Letting the savage win would mean her destruction.

Everything inside him revolted over the prospect. Above all else, Flint needed to stay alive to help her. "So help me, I will be here for you...Darlin'"

CHAPTER 11
Camouflage

Her steps along the deer path were heavy in their sure course. The long wait for him to leave took away the night she'd hoped to have to catch up to Flint. The threat still remained before her. The Indian didn't give up, he'd only delayed the time when they would meet again.

Jolene couldn't shake the doubt Awasos left in his wake. Flint, how she worried over him. He would know that she followed, regardless of what it might mean to her. Her lip grew sore over the nervous bites she'd given it. Flint would be furious and her stomach knotted over the truth of just how angry he could become.

Jolene tried not to think about what the future held for Flint and herself. She concentrated on following the deer path. She'd waited nearly three hours before moving after last seeing Awasos searching for her on the rise. It looked as if he wanted her to see his search, he moved openly around the mountain face after swimming back across the river. She knew when he'd left, but she'd been unable to find the courage to follow too closely. Jolene feared this new opponent more than anything that happened to her since that summer storm...so long ago.

Only Flint and what he meant to her kept her headed into the eminent danger awaiting her arrival. Somehow she would find a way to beat that man before his trap fell upon her.

The morning held more than the light and warmth that made her exhaustion ease. Again she'd found the deserted camp and the trail. The blatant evidence of their passing left her cold in warning. Awasos wanted to make it easy for her. The ill feelings intensified during the morning. Her own open movements over the trail were almost in defiance to what she would soon face. The apprehension inside Jolene almost made her miss the signs that their pace changed. The discovery made Jolene's instincts snap and drive her into the woods, off the worn path now under foot.

Finding cover she shrank down onto the forest floor, needing the time to gather her thoughts. Her thinking cleared, taking away the smothering fear that stayed with her all morning. The scent of smoke caressed her open senses to the path where many feet walked into what was probably their village.

Her sharp sight found the rise that would tell her. But something held her back from going to it. The man knew she would come. Jolene decided she better rethink all the normal courses of action to avoid what undoubtedly waited for her expected arrival.

A mischievous smile took away her troubled frown, "I've got nothing to lose."

Oh God, Jolene, you are insane to be doing this. For the hundredth time she told her feet to move normally as she walked past another cooking fire and women tending them. The heavy lengths of their doeskin skirts slapped against the leggings of her moccasins beneath the stolen folds. Clutching the wrap tighter about her chin, she bemoaned the hidden shortness of her ash dirtied hair. It was the only thing, besides her blue eyes, all her watching of the village women couldn't compensate for. The wool shawl she'd stolen seemed the only way to hide the difference the clothes couldn't conceal.

All afternoon she studied the comings and goings of the women…and men, from her hiding place. Awasos drew her awareness almost immediately. His awesome carriage walked as a dominant presence among the people, telling boldly of the obvious position he held in their lives. The knowledge he was their chief almost defeated Jolene's resolve to do what she decided. Only walking freely among them would allow her to find Flint when her search from the perimeter failed to locate him. Somewhere behind one of these hide and bark huts is where she would find him.

Disguising herself as one of their women gave her the freedom to search. At least she'd entered the camp. Picking up the water jug, she tried to appear as casual as her nerves allowed. Keeping her eyes averted from the braves that came near her, she managed to avoid being discovered. Moving slowly through the village she hoped her meandering didn't draw attention as she looked for some sign of a guard that would indicate Flint's presence. The village was larger than she'd ever imagined they could be.

When she'd moved through half of it, Jolene began to worry that they might have taken him somewhere else. She couldn't keep daring fate by her continued presence. The way two braves began watching her sent a chill up her spine. Moving with more purpose towards the river she hoped they would lose interest.

Sinking down into the gravel bank and dipping the jug under the water, she scanned for an area she might have missed. Instead, Awasos filled her vision. His purposeful strides ahead of two braves held her mesmerized.

Pulling the jug up, Jolene knew she must take the chance, he could be going to Flint. Trying to catch up to them, she was practically running. The cold stares following her passing made her slow in warning.

Awasos stopped before a hut, making Jolene duck behind the one next to it. He issued orders to the two men, making her certain Flint must be behind the stark hardness ruling the man's action. He sent two men about the back of the hut, adding to the guards already in place about the opening.

She needed to get inside.

Before Jolene could decide what to do more men and a woman started coming about the open area in front of the hut. Before her startled gaze the drummers came out of nowhere and began a cold threatening beat that filled her with foreboding. The reason for the gathering screamed inside her head until her heart pounded in rhythm to the horrible drums. "Flint, no...please no."

Anger blazed in the depths of her soul against the man now issuing orders to some woman. This would be her only chance.

Jolene moved out into the crowd, her step never faltered as she walked boldly up to the hut. She never looked at the growing mass of people behind her. Awasos's closeness pricked at her senses.

Never acknowledging the guards she walked between them, hesitating only a second. When no hands or sharp words came to stop her she bent down and entered the confines of the hovel.

The only light came from a small fire in the center, but her eyes would have found him regardless of the darkness. An animalistic groan welled up inside her for the gashes and welts marring his proud body. The sound of Awasos's voice above the drums snapped Jolene into action.

Spanning the distance to him, his lack of awareness to her presence terrified her more than his wounds. Fearing what he might do when he realized her presence, Jolene raised her hand and covered his mouth. His eyes flashed in all their startled rage directly into her own. "Please love, not a sound."

Her heart screamed until he finally answered with a nod of recognition. Taking the knife Jolene cut away the rawhide binding his arms to the pole over his head. She kept to her task and moved quickly down to cut away the ones about his chest, legs and feet.

The clasp of his hand shoving back the shawl made her raise her head up to look into his eyes. "Flint..."

"Oh God, why Jolene, why did you come?"

Her lips silenced the pain she heard. "Shh, there's no time."

Pulling away from him nearly made her tears fall. Sticking the knife into the wall of hides she silently brought it down, creating the opening he would need. Jolene knew what she must do, what he would fight her over. She talked close to his ear, knowing he struggled just to stay conscious. While she told him the layout of the village she slipped the knife into his belt. Their time disappeared. "Flint, can you make it?"

"I will."

"There are two guards at the back and two in front. They won't be long in coming for you."

"I heard." His hand closed about her wrist, and she closed her eyes over what she feared from him.

"No Flint, you have to go alone. They saw me come in here and if I don't leave they'll be coming in. The river is to the north, there are canoes there, take one. I'll meet you by the fork to the southwest."

"Jolene..."

The cold warning made her head shake to defy him. "Go."

Before he could stop her Jolene left him and went to the door. In her haste to leave and make him go she almost forgot to pull the shawl up. Flint needed time. His lack of strength to keep her beside him told her just how injured he must be.

Coming to her feet outside the hut she moved, determined to make sure he received the time he needed to reach the river. She didn't think his escape would go unnoticed for very long.

Head down she moved pass the guards and into the crowd.

CHAPTER 12
Heartfelt acts

Something familiar touched Awasos about the figure leaving the hut. Shaking his head to clear away the ridiculous thought, he lost sight of her in the crowd. A slow throbbing anger stole over him, sending a ripple of awareness through his body.

Jolene nearly cried out over the furious shout coming from Awasos, like lightening clashing in the air! Unable to stop herself she stopped and turned to find him. He stood there searching for her in the crowd. Turning away Jolene ducked into the first hut she came to. A sigh of relief flooded out when she found it was empty. Taking a burning stick from the cooking fire she went about the hut lighting the dry bark. Making sure the arson caught she tossed the flaming stick into the robes. The startled cry came so slight she almost failed to hear it. Arguing with herself, Jolene ran to the furs pulling them away. "Oh God."

The dark haired baby stared up at her, kicking his chubby feet in excited gurgles. The smoke assaulted her nostrils. "Come on little fella', you will probably never forgive me for what I almost did, but at least God didn't let me hurt you."

Clutching the child, Jolene ran from the inferno that flashed to life about them.

Awasos saw the small figure running away from the hut before it burst into flames. Ready to charge after her, her next act halted his purpose. Watching as she carefully placed the infant down in front of another wigwam, his chest swelled, his conviction over her proved right. That courageous spirit was ruled by a stronger innate gentleness. It forbade her from hurting another, even for feelings as strong as she held for the white scout.

As if she heard his thoughts she turned to meet Awasos's figure across the distance. The flames licking the night danced across his dark chest. His legs were spread wide in threat, making her stumble back. Before he could move, Jolene's legs were running. The shawl fell away, its necessity no longer important. He was coming for her, as she always knew he would since his words at the river.

"The river!" Groaning, Jolene abruptly changed her course, never could she take him to the river, to Flint!

Awasos sent his men in the direction she'd veered away from, instinctively knowing what she'd just told him. The chase and girl he pursued were for him alone to take to the finish.

Gaining the woods Jolene never slowed her escape, scaling bushes and darting past trees it didn't matter where her flight took her...he was coming!

With every footfall Flint's battered body tortured her memory. She prayed that Flint would get away. The heavy steps gaining on her told Jolene of her own failure to escape. The growl from directly behind her made her scream, but the steel hold jerking her back off her feet into the iron wall of his chest made the fear die in her lungs. The race against who held her from reaching Flint sent her arms and legs striking out in fury. "Nooo...Oh God, make him let go!" Though she refused to quit, Jolene knew she'd lost to the power catching and ending her struggles in an unbreakable capture.

Pulling her fully against his frame Awasos' locked her to his thigh. Her fight nearly took away all the ash from her hair. The blazing wisps floated wildly about his head and neck assaulting his nostrils, infusing his victory over her. As she stilled under his pinning hold the sensual ripples of her abating rage drove a fierce awakening though Awasos's pulsing veins. Touching her was like coming too close to the sun's power and the truth seared his male senses. He admired her skills and abilities before her cunning this night, but at the moment all Awasos felt was the womanly essence she possessed.

Jolene squeezed her eyes shut to fight the overpowering closeness of his body. In shocking boldness every taunt detail burned past the flimsy barriers of clothes to her sensitive flesh. His hold forbade any separation, struggling proved useless. Waging a war against her own frightened emotions she tried to calm herself, even if it only made him stop touching her.

Her breasts still pulsed from the exertion they'd just been through. Awasos felt her womanly buds grow tight and harden with each tantalizing brush against his bare chest. He brought her closer, pressing her small curved hips into the evidence of his intention. The weakening tremble racing through her made his excitement soar for what he would claim.

"Your fear is like a sweet nectar in my blood."

Her renewed struggles to break away only made him grind hard against her womanly pelt until she stopped. Her breath fell in frightened gasp across his fevered flesh. "Your courage and spirit won't keep me from taking you upon my pallet. Nor will your white scout. He will soon face what you freed him from this night."

"You won't find him." Her faith hissed out, making the man grip her chin in his course hold.

"And if I do not, maybe you should take his place." Her eyes looked like the steeled blades of the white's knives. "You'd even die to protect him."

He searched her eyes for the confirmation. What it did to him drove him from her. But his breaking hold about her wrist didn't release her fully. Dragging her along beside him, her struggles to get free never relented. His determination to exert his right on this captive grew in intensity. He wanted to crush what she dared to show him!

When they reentered the village, it ran alive with excitement. Jolene feared they'd found Flint. Awasos pulled her along against her futile struggles. A group of braves came running towards them, Awasos stopped and waited. Jolene took the chance, leaning forward she bit his hand.

The release came, but so did the back of his hand across her face, sending her to her knees before him. The brutal hold on her hair kept her down. All she could see were legs encircling her. Tasting the blood at her swollen lips lent evidence to the brutality she could face at his hands. The truth stilled her fight, but built the fires of rage over the injustice she would soon be forced to face.

There wasn't any shouting in his orders that sent the others away. When he forced her up to her feet by his cruel pull on her hair, she came to face the anger barring down at her. Her triumph grew too great to keep silent, "He's free!"

Jerking her against him, his other arm held her fast. "But you are not! A fair trade, but your payment will be high."

Jolene tried hard not to show what his vicious vow did to her.

She suffered his wrath in his harsh hold as he led her through the village to his lodge. The log structure looked larger than any she'd seen.

Pushing her before him through the door he dragged her across the large room.

Jolene feared he meant to carry out his ugly threat and renewed her fight against his hold.

Capturing her wrist, Awasos ended their striking blows, tying them tight behind her back. Pushing her down on the pallet he loomed over her. Those crystal eyes grew large over what he knew she expected. Taking his finger he traced the parted lips and watched as she trembled like a fawn in his sights. "Your fear of me is justified little white scout, but when I take you there will be no need for bonds. I'll take you and all your fury, but in the end you will be mine."

Pulling his finger away before her sharp teeth could capture it, his low laughter made her try and turn away from him. Moving his hand down the smooth curve of her hip, down her leg when they moved to avoid his caress, Awasos held and bound them as well. Taking hold of her hair he made her look at him. "He won't save you, there is no hide to slit to reach you and the guards won't allow anyone to pass. I won't be gone long."

Jolene didn't move until she heard the door close on his receding footsteps. Turning towards the wall she brought her knees up to her stomach to fend off the terrible horrors. "Oh Flint, please be safe, I won't survive if you aren't."

CHAPTER 13
False Beliefs

"The southwest fork..." Blocking out all other sensations Flint concentrated on raising his arms to force the paddle through the water. The pain searing his flesh and mind weren't allowed to interfere with reaching the spot she spoke of and finding Jolene. She must be there, he refused to believe otherwise.

Guiding the canoe towards the left fork, the current picked up taking him forward. Using the paddle to steady the speeding canoe, the stilling motion allowed him to hear the slapping sound that spoke of his pursuers.

They could have noticed the missing canoe, but the nagging suspicion that their pursuit had more do with Jolene intensified. His fear for her gave him the strength their tortures stole. Using the last of his energy Flint went against the current, forcing the canoe to the right fork. Once he reached the mouth he deliberately tipped the canoe, sending it into the rocks.

Flint let the current take him. He didn't begin to swim to shore until he was well down the eastern branch. Gaining the shore, he used the hanging branches to pull himself up and out of the water. Hiding there, he used the time to revitalize his strength, while he watched to see if they believed his ploy. They knew what kind of condition he was in and should believe that he'd drown.

"Awasos!" Flint's hate hissed out over the man in the lead canoe. Every violent instinct told him that man captured Jolene. Their Chief's lack of anger over loosing Flint as a captive sealed Flint's dreaded conviction.

Flint couldn't afford to waste any time to reach her.

"Lies! Stop it!" Jolene covered her ears and tried not to listen to the torment.

Awasos wasn't going to let her carry the hope for her scout beyond tonight. "He drown in his flight."

No, she wouldn't believe his cruel words. He just wanted to hurt her.

Holding her hands above her head Awasos studied the young, soft features closed against him. The fine proud lines were so vulnerable now. Before the sun rose, she would know only his touch upon her ermine skin. His finger traced the evidence of his mark in the marring bruise. It wasn't something he wanted to see again, but she would learn not to defy him.

The firm hold about her jaw made her eyes open against the warnings. The tightening clasp about her wrist made Jolene's efforts to pull free seem like a sparrow fighting the hawk.

"The hope still fuels your will to fight what I will be to you. Shall I show you?"

His hand slid down the pulsing column of her neck until it reached the rawhide strip holding her blouse together. In agonizing slowness she felt him pull the leather strips through the holes. "Don't do this to me!"

The half smile he gave her made her regret speaking out. He enjoyed her weakness.

"Words won't stop me from taking what has been mine since the river."

"I wish...."

"You'd let me drown? Ah, little scout, hurting another is beyond your vast abilities. It is a weakness I am sure you regret."

His hand slipped beneath the doeskin covering the firm globes of her breasts. The weight of his body over her own made the struggles she waged useless. When he took the hardened nipple between his fingers, her anguish turned into a song of defeat. But Awasos wanted her full submission and grew impatient to feel the passion he knew she possessed.

The release of her hands became fleeting freedom. In the same instant he gripped the collar of her shirt, forcefully bringing it down over her shoulders and breasts, to her waist, trapping her arms tight within the garment.

Leaning back as he straddled her slim waist his heated gaze couldn't get enough of the exposed beauty. White as a snow owl, the mounds rose and fell brazenly before him. The dark teats were earthy, inflaming his savage lust.

Holding them, he let the weight fill his palms.

Make him stop! But her plea went unanswered, intensifying the fears over his words that Flint truly died in the river.

When the weight lifted from her body, Jolene's mind became numb to what would follow. Flint...her life, without him she didn't care what happened, she wouldn't live without Flint! Whatever the man did to her couldn't be as bad as the pain in her heart.

Seeing her half naked beneath that gloating bastard blinded Flint in internal rage!

Pulling the savage away from her the knife sliced the air in deadly meaning, sending the man stumbling back across the room. "I told you I'd kill you."

The desire still burning in his loins for the woman on his furs dulled Awasos's senses to her man's entrance and the threat slashing dangerously before him. Pulling out his own knife, his body straightened in readiness for the next attack. The vicious speed and velocity coming from the man stunned Awasos. The bleeding evidence of his battered body had no effect on the man's skill with the knife.

Vengeful fury drove Flint wildly at the man. His blade's accuracy cut a fine line across the bronze stomach. The surprise in those dark eyes increased Flint's taste for blood. In reckless pursuit he drove him back into the wall, lunging at him their holds locked in the death struggle. Flint's blade inched towards the man's face cutting into his cheek. Sounding like a wounded animal the Indian's painful surge of strength broke Flint's hold. Falling back he moved to the side just as the savage flew through the air. A hard silencing whack made the Indian's body stay down.

Rolling the unmoving Awasos over, Flint saw the blow on his forehead where it hit one of the rocks about the cooking fire. Raising his knife to finish the job, the horrible groan from behind him made him spin around.

Jolene came up on her knees, holding herself as if she'd fall apart before his eyes.

"Darlin'!" Rushing to her, the horror enlarging her eyes made her rock. "Oh God, Jolene it's me."

"Lies! So cruel...all lies! You are wrong, he is not dead!"

Gathering her in his arms, her fists beat weakly against his body.

"I don't care what you do to me if he is dead. I am too!"

His hand stilled her violent shaking. His rage over what happened to her wouldn't be stilled, but Jolene's needs came before any others. "Darlin', it's me, Flint."

Holding her tear stained face Flint made her look at him. "I'm here love. Come on Jolene see me."

"Flint?"

"Yes, Darlin', you didn't believe that savage could kill me, now did you?"

Her head shook like a small child, fighting with the need to believe. When her shaking fingers came up to touch his face, he remained still.

"Oh my...it is you."

His lips parted beneath her palm in relief. With the strength he feared might be stolen from her, she flung her arms about his neck in a fierce hold that buried her into his own unbreakable embrace. The dangers still surrounding them wouldn't allow them more than a moment.

"Jolene, we must go." His whisper made her grow stiff in his arms. When she pulled back, the shame that made her struggle to cover herself turned into a suffering he never wanted her to experience. His guilt for failing to protect Jolene loomed before him. He bore it in silence, the gnawing rage holding tight inside his gut couldn't be allowed to hurt her any further.

CHAPTER 14
Love Hurts

"**I** never doubted you would be back."

McKean's hand slapped Flint's back. "We're relieved you suffered no harm..."

Jolene met Flint's gaze above the heads in the crowd, Flint's still held that distance she'd come to recognize during the journey back from Awasos's village. She bit the inside of her cheek to hold back from showing these people anything beyond what they wanted to see. Unable to continue the charade she slipped away from the celebration, needing to find the familiar feelings their camp always held.

Jolene fell into the troubled thoughts that somehow became a part of her these last days on the trail. Flint became obsessed with getting them away and putting distance between the wagons and the Iroquois; in truth, from Awasos.

Sighing, she learned Awasos wasn't dead, though the blow would have killed another it wouldn't be enough for that man. The fear she tried to bury because of him wouldn't settle.

Closing her eyes Jolene fought back the plaguing tears that threatened to overwhelm her out on the trail. Being back here seemed to bring it all back. They could no longer use the constant urgency to avoid their pursuers as an excuse to block out what now stood between them. Like an insurmountable wall, the distance grew between Flint and Jolene until she feared never to be able to span it and reach Flint.

When she first caught his unguarded gaze on her, what she witnessed in those cold blue torrents shocked her. It didn't take her long to realize what caused the vicious anger he didn't want her to see. It made Jolene's own shameful hurt almost unbearable. A strange, almost violent denial came over her then. What caused Flint's rage never happened!

Yes, she'd always carry the scars of the man who had assaulted and humiliated her, but the final act of his cruelty wasn't committed. Flint's belief that it happened could be the only reason for the cold ravage of pain reflected in his eyes; ones that no longer seemed to hold any warmth for her.

Shivering against the memory, Jolene failed to correct what he must have seen when entering Awasos's lodge. "Oh Flint, I tried, why won't you listen."

She went to him, seeing that he appeared lost in his tortured thoughts she reached out and touched his arm. His unexpected retaliation really hadn't been against her, she'd seen that too in the pain filling his face over the fierce hold he used against her. When he set her from him instead of holding her, is when the cold daggers stabbed through her heart. Rebelling against the pain she tried to tell him.

"Flint, please don't, it..." Why the right words failed to come, is something she will never forget. "he...please Flint, I..."

His hands took hold of her arms in a cruel hold that's force made her head rattle. "Don't Jolene! Don't ever speak of it again! If you have any feelings left for us, let it stay buried back where we left it!"

She felt his words hammer their finality into her bruised heart, leaving her shattered and lost. The terrible silence that started then followed them and intensified into the distance he now kept between them. So many times she tried to build her courage to make him listen. But it was like he knew her intentions before she could instigate a confrontation and his fierce, hardened glare would close all paths of communication.

Being here, touching their things, having him safe should make it all right. But Jolene found no comfort and despaired over the man, her husband that now looked at her as a cold stranger.

"Mrs. Flint?"

The small voice made Jolene jump, startling the boy behind her. If she looked and felt miserable the little boy with overly bright blue eyes looked devastated. Holding her arms out to him, "Oh David! Come here love, I missed you so much."

Any hesitation over her proclamation was lost in the relief that sent him flying into her arms.

Flint held back from intruding on the scene between them. He didn't think those tears came for the same reasons. Maybe Jolene needed the boy to help take her mind away from the horror.

His frame vibrated under the weight of anger that couldn't find a release. His lips firmed over the decision not to ever let her beg his forgiveness as she'd tried out on the trail. Seeing and knowing how much she hurt, he couldn't allow her to shame herself anymore. *I should have gone back and slit the savage's throat.*

But getting her away before the alarms went off in the village took priority. Flint knew what he'd face if he failed again. His fingers closed over the hilt of his knife in remembered conviction that blurred her image. Taking a steadying breath, thankfully he hadn't been forced to commit that travesty against her. In his heart he knew if it ever came to letting that bastard get his hands on her again, his own brutality in taking her life would be a blessing driven by love.

Raising his eyes to the stars, he swore again she'd not suffer anymore. For Jolene, he would do whatever it took to keep her safe. He couldn't slay the ugly memories, but he could force them out of their lives. He told himself again he would give her all the time necessary to heal. Until she did his own touch would not rekindle the terror.

Firm in his belief, Flint entered the camp.

She saw him before David did.

"Is that your famous rabbit stew I smell David?"

The blonde head nodded against her breasts. Jolene couldn't make herself meet Flint's gaze. The tears still wet her cheeks.

"Come on you two, I'm starved."

When the boy moved and Flint filled his vision, Jolene felt the flight enter his body.

Jolene tried to ease the boy's fears. "Rabbit stew sounds real good." Covering her own surprise over Flint's obvious cordiality for David, Jolene spoke up, "Then we'd best all eat before we waste away. David would you get the bowls?"

"Yes ma'am."

Throughout their dinner the two males gave each other cautious looks, it started to be almost amusing to watch. Jolene decided it must be her own uncertainty regarding Flint's unexpected attitude towards the boy that kept her constant chatter flowing.

Something was going on behind those dark blue eyes that eluded her. All she could hold on to is that the coldness wasn't in Flint's features any longer. A tiny flicker of hope? Jolene prayed it to be so.

She made David help her with dishes to keep him in camp. The chill in the air made her worry over the boy. When there were no more chores, she resigned herself to his leaving. But Flint seemed bent on filling the evening with surprises.

"Boy...I set a place up under the wagon for you. It's late, best you get to bed."

Flint never turned from feeding the fire with fresh logs to see David's mouth drop open. When he looked at her, Jolene's silent nod and push sent him to get into the blankets.

Pushing her own indecision away, Jolene walked over and sat down beside Flint at the fire. Afraid to question the change in him, she stared at the dancing flames shooting sparks up into the blackness.

"When it gets colder he is going to have to sleep in the wagon."

Keeping her eyes on the fire proved hard over what he'd just implied.

"You better get to bed, too, Jolene."

Damn, she hated the uncertainty she felt. Rising because she couldn't find any excuse not to. "Will you be in soon?"

If only he'd look at her.

"I need to check on a few things first."

"Alright Flint." Jolene started towards the wagon. Stopping, she didn't turn back to him. "Thank you Flint."

He listened to her getting up into the wagon and settling down before he rose to go.

"Whatever it takes, Darlin.'"

CHAPTER 15
Enough is Enough!

The weeks passed since their return. They fell back into a routine. Only Jolene seemed concerned by the changes. One brought happiness into her heart.

David became a part of their lives. Though Flint could still be reserved around the boy, he did little things that gave Jolene faith in their relationship developing into something more.

The first came by the moccasins that appeared one morning beside the campfire. She'd seen Flint watching the boy's reaction to them from the wagon. That David walked around proud of his footwear was an understatement. The knife and fur cap that followed in the same manner sent him boasting all over camp.

The fact David tagged determinedly after Flint made Jolene's hope hard to keep quiet. Everyday Flint's stern aloofness concerning David seemed to crack a little more. David became as determined to get the man, now in his life, to accept him as Flint attempted to keep him at arm's length. This morning she felt an unprecedented action by David stumped her husband.

David stepped boldly in front of Flint before he could leave, "I want to go with you to scout ahead today. The other men go. I want to do my part."

Jolene held her breath to see what would happen. Flint's expression never changed as he studied the boy standing before him. "Have Jolene fix you a satchel."

It was all David could do not to jump in excitement.

When Flint turned and looked at her, the unbidden smile coming over her made his head shake in resignation.

Jolene fixed up the boy's lunch, while he raced around in nervous haste gathering everything he'd need. "Should I take the pistol?"

She barely hid her surprise. "No David."

"But..."

"What's wrong?" She adjusted the leather strap over his chest for the satchel.

"What if the Indians jump us?"

Keeping the fear out of her gaze and voice took all her control. "You just do everything Flint tells you, without question."

"I promise."

"Go on now, he's waiting."

The unexpected hug about her neck left a lump in Jolene's throat. If only the man watching would do the same. Fighting back the tears, she started to put things away to get ready to move out. But her acts held no thought, no, they were all on Flint.

Since that first night back, nothing changed beyond David. Flint came in late to the wagon. She hadn't been able to sleep, knowing because she waited for him. But the arm she longed to feel about her never came. Oh, he slept in the same cot, beside her, but never did he touch her beyond the forced closeness, not even just to hold her in sleep.

Once they woke in each other's arms. Flint looked so upset she moved away instead of clinging to him like she wanted to do. The error never got repeated. She almost doubted he ever actually slept to prevent a reoccurrence.

If shame were a living beast it swallowed her in its ravenous hunger. All logic told her Flint could never hate her for what happened. But his aversion to touch her said blame did get placed, deliberately or not. Another man touched what should be his alone.

Jolene tried to reverse their roles, but failed miserably. Forgive! Forgive! It was all she could hear. That she wanted to ask forgiveness for what never happened became a horrible lie to live with.

Everything she'd ever read about rape came back to her. Nothing helped take away the pain his actions inflicted. In truth, Flint hurt her more than Awasos ever could have...only Flint could break her heart.

Cursing that she let her thoughts touch on that horrible man brought a chill over her. Other things changed. No longer did she enter the woods. In fact, she rarely stepped a foot out of camp since their return. David or Flint fetched the wood and water. At first Flint just took it over. Just like he stopped setting up their camp at a distance from the others. But Jolene knew her own fear held her back from stopping him.

She made herself block out the terror every time he left camp. Now David went with him. Jolene couldn't let the frightened feelings overtake her. At least Flint no longer scouted alone.

Laughing nervously to herself she rechecked the oxen harnesses. "More surprises."

McKean actually instigated that change. No, he commanded past Flint's objections that at least one man if not two be with him on every excursion.

Flint's temper took almost a week to settle down against the man. Begrudgingly, a side benefit appeared that finally cooled Flint's ire. The men unexpectedly became avid and apt learners. So much so that Flint started taking on the role of teacher to his apprentices. She thought Flint felt really pleased by their progress. His worry over how these people would survive found an outlet to change what he couldn't stop.

Everything around them seemed to be going better. Her grandfather would say the kinks were getting straightened out.

Jolene spent the whole day alone to think on how to sort out her own tangled mess. And as the oxen started their untroubled pace she set her mind to the task. Somehow she needed to find a way to let Flint know she never suffered the final assault of rape.

How could she get through the barriers he erected? Dare she try?

Jolene kicked at a small rock, of course she must tell him. Everything told her that Flint would continue to distance himself from her unless she could tear down that wall. "So help me Flint, you are going to listen to me...you must, my love."

She could hear David's excited voice coming closer to their camp. She wondered if he would ever unwind from his day with Flint. Jolene felt her impatience; she took a deep breath to calm her nerves. She told herself again that her plan needed to be done. She closed her eyes and said a quick prayer that everything would be fine.

"Jolene!" She turned just in time to catch David as he ran to her. The boy's excited words flew one after another.

Flint watched the boy tell Jolene all about his adventure, but he only heard the joy in her laughter. He realized how long it had been since her laughter filled the air. God, but he did miss her. He missed the smell of her filling his senses when he returned to camp. Flint wanted the touch of her arms around his neck and the warm feel of her lips on his. He needed to hold her and tell her how much he loved her, but he couldn't allow his wants and needs to take precedence.

She watched the emotions moving across his proud face, and she wanted to scream when the distance once again fell in place. If she were a man she'd go right up to him... "Oh heck, what do I have to lose! Get something to eat David, this may take a while."

Flint started to leave, but Jolene refused to let him, "Oh no you don't, Mr. Allen Flint!"

She almost plowed into his back when he stopped dead in his tracks. When he didn't turn to face her she gripped his arm and made him turn and look at her. For a second Jolene wondered what she would do if this didn't work.

"You need to stay here!"

"Jolene..."

"No!" Her foot stomped. "We need to get something straight between us and I refuse to wait any longer for you to...to, want me again."

His mouth started to open then snapped shut, and she almost growled at him. Not even that cold stare would make her stop now. "Yes Allen, want me!" Her fist pounded her chest for emphasis. "I love you Allen, with all my heart and I want you to love me again. I can't stand this cold wall of indifference you keep between us. It is killing us Allen!"

"Jolene, I..."

"No! No more excuses to leave, no more late nights without sleep so you won't touch me!" She fought back the tears threatening to fall. "I didn't get raped Allen. He never got that far, you stopped him...Oh Allen, you stopped him and saved me...I would have died if you'd been killed, do you know that?

But you were there, and you stopped him and all the cruel things he said about you being dead weren't true."

Flint reached out and wiped the tears from her cheeks, his own fell in abandon. "Darlin'..."

"Oh yes, yes Flint, you still love me don't you?" He finally called her Darlin' and Jolene felt herself go weak in joy.

He caught her as she moved towards him and nearly fell. "It's alright Darlin' I'm so sorry, I thought..."

Her hand covered his lips, "It never happened Allen. I'm so sorry I didn't tell you right off, I tried, I did, but the words just got all messed up and I failed you, I did and I'm sorry. Please forgive me Allen. I love you so much."

"Darlin'?"

"Yes?"

"You can stop now, I'm finally listening to you." He smiled down into her tear stained face. "I'm the fool here, Jolene. You tried to tell me and I let my damnable pride prevent me from hearing you." He felt her fingers digging into his back as if she could hold him to her forever. "I love you Darlin'."

"Oh Allen, my dear sweet husband, please kis...."

She never got the chance to finish. Flint's lips took hers and the moment they touched all his desire took over. It was Jolene that finally made them break apart. The look he gave her made her laughter float on the breeze. "Come on Allen, come with me."

Jolene called out to David to stoke the fire and get to bed, they'd be back in a while. Flint followed her into the woods, and she just kept going for the longest time. He almost started to stop her when she finally called a halt. When she stepped to his side, he saw what she led him to. There, under the cloaking tree branches lay a blanket and a basket with food, she even thought of a lantern. He looked at her, and she gave him a smile that spoke of the wonders ahead.

"I figured out why you always set up our camp away from the others."

When he started laughing she joined him and his arms went around her, lifting her up off the ground and Flint swung her around and around!

He kept hold of her when he lowered her feet back to the ground. Words weren't necessary; she already started to undo the ties of her dress. Flint rid himself of his clothes, he wanted to feel her lovely beauty against his hard flesh.

Yet when she stood naked before him, bathed in shimmering moonlight he couldn't stop looking at his Darlin'. "You fill my heart Jolene. I never thought I could feel so much love for a woman."

She stepped towards him with a gentle smile on her lips. "I'm all yours Allen, I will never love another, never my sweet husband."

Their vows spoken as if for the first time, their bodies melded as one. When Flint lifted her up before him, her legs wrapped about his waist, and she found the swollen head of his sex. She held onto his shoulders and let him guide her down over the pulsing shaft so long denied. Once sheathed within her velvet folds, he could feel the excitement racing through her. She arched, Flint's hands spread out across her back to hold her as passion ruled.

Jolene's body danced over him under the moonlight. She rode him to excite and stimulate the fierce nature that men try not to let loose, but his Darlin' wanted what Flint tried to tame. She deliberately coaxed the wild exotic part of him to join her and when his hold tightened she purred sweetly in victory as he thrust her down to take in the full erotic length until Flint kissed the very womb of his woman!

His cry joined hers and their joining rose to a fierce pitch of sweet ecstasy, and he gloried in the vibrant passion she showed him, the feral depth of her desire to have him inside her wet wanton sex. The sure presence of her need as she drove herself down the full potent length again and again, until Flint thought he'd explode. Oh, but she wanted him to do just that, and she rode him as a woman possessed in her mission to satisfy the beast held captive in her wanton prison.

Flint's cry of victory spread out through the darkness as he held her to him, so that each powerful burst of his release drove into the very depth of her sex. Together they held on to each other wanting the luxury to be endless and intimacy to last forever...

CHAPTER 16
Danger all around

Holding the boy's arm Flint guided them back from the rocks. The lad was smart, nodding silently over Flint's hand command to head back to the others and away from the threat they'd stumbled upon.

The alert cobalt eyes kept guard over their retreat away from the full contingent of French militia and their massacring companions. Jolene's words came back cold in their naked threat over the scene beneath the rise. The Iroquois and French together, it appeared to be an obvious admission of their evil intent, one no arguments could disguise.

Thankfully the other men from camp were waiting at the designated spot. Flint wasted little in way of words and time in explaining the danger less than a mile ahead. Getting back to the others held their urgency.

The rage he'd carried these last weeks rose to the surface in shocking speed. He must reach Jolene. His jaw clenched over the man he'd not seen among them. Flint's gut told him it wasn't much of a guarantee. Awasos could already have found her.

Word spread quickly over the danger that could strike the settlers at any moment. Jolene's absence from the gathering crowd sent Flint from McKean's side. He didn't realize David was still beside him until he saw the boy running to keep up. Flint's impatience made him pick up the boy and swing him up onto his back.

"She's alright, isn't she?"

How could he answer the boy? Was it only his own fear that drove him like a mad man to find her.

Racing into the camp, Flint slowed.

Jolene was fixing dinner.

Easing David down to the ground the need to hold her overwhelmed all his caution. Coming up behind her, he wrapped his arms around her waist. "Hmm, you smell good Darlin.'"

It was all she could do not to throw herself into his arms. All her control fell away before the man looking down at her. "I need you so much, Allen Flint."

Heaven could only be these strong arms holding her off the ground against him. Her own found their hold about his neck, her fingers threaded into the thick rich gold waves. "I love you Allen." They were the only words she could find to explain all she held inside so long.

"Oh Darlin', I know."

"Just hold me, always hold me. I think I'll die if you shut me away again."

He had been such a fool to have done this to her. "God Jolene, I swear I'll listen to you, no matter what."

Her fingers touched his lips. Looking up at him, she smiled, "I know, Allen."

If it was relief that softened his firm face, she wanted to mourn its short life. "Flint? Please love...tell me...."

But his lips never allowed the pleas to be voiced. She thought he'd crush her in the fierce hold that came over him. In an instant those warm unforgotten lips were gone and her misty eyes searched for answers.

"I have a penance for starting what can't be completed with you."

Was he actually smiling?

Her head unconsciously cocked to the side in bewilderment. She shouldn't have any doubts about him after their night in the woods. Seeing that the wall did indeed crumble, she wasn't about to let the first brick be righted. And she brazenly told him so, "the wagon is the best, Mr. Simons assured me..."

Her meaning came clear enough to send a red flush up those proud cheeks. Just to insure she crushed any lingering doubts. "If it falls off its axis, I'll be the first in the colonies to sue the man for poor workmanship."

Taking hold of his hand Jolene started to lead him towards the suspect vehicle. When his unmovable form pulled her back, Jolene felt a tightness in her throat.

"Darlin', you have no idea how much I want to test Mr. Simon's workmanship. Though I do have a taste for the woods..." Flint wasn't beyond teasing her about their night of wild loving under the stars, anything to stop the dulling in her smiling face. When that smoldering passion flared over to anger, Flint locked her hard against the truth of his desire. Holding her trim hips he slowly moved her over the undeniable evidence of just how badly he wanted this volatile lady.

Sucking in her breath, her fingers closed over the virile evidence of his erection. She leaned her head back and their gazes locked.

God, he hated to end this, but he could hear McKean shouting orders to the men. He felt Jolene's body stiffen as her hand slipped away from him, she heard them too.

The passion fell away from the violet depths searching his for answers.

"We came across a company of French militia...."

Her fingers dug into his arm, and he nodded over the question she couldn't speak.

"Yes, the Iroquois were there."

Flint's hands held her up under the sudden weakness that buckled her knees.

"I'll be okay Flint."

Her control was something that still amazed him. "It will be alright, Jolene."

She couldn't answer, just nodding. This wasn't Awasos's village. She was surrounded by her own people...and Flint.

"Jolene, I want you and the boy to get the rifle and pistols loaded. Take the barrels and large pots off the wagon and place them around the wagon for a shield. Neither of you are to leave from under the wagon unless I say so."

She wasn't sure if she could even try for lightness to ease his concern for her. "Nothing will dislodge us, I swear."

Flint tucked his finger under her chin. "We can give David the wagon...later."

Hearing McKean calling for Flint, she reached up and held him, close to his ear she whispered. "I don't care when or where my dear husband, just as long as we're together."

CHAPTER 17
Vengeance

Waiting made the anticipation of the attack unbearable. Having David curled up at her side gave Jolene a reason not to give in to the awful thoughts.

"It is so quiet."

"Hmm." Her fingers played with his hair. She could hear David's fear in his whisper. "Why don't you tell me about why you were alone?"

Neither of them ever talked about it. "David you don't have to worry, you belong here with us now."

"I know."

"Never mind, it doesn't matter."

No, Flint's acceptance of the boy said it would be fine.

"She died on the ship."

Jolene's fingers stopped, lying protectively on his head. "I'm so sorry, David."

"She was a good person, not like some that came over. My father died a long time back. People told my mother that over here a man would accept a woman with a child. That's why she did it."

She could feel his small body actually ease over the words spilling out.

"I just hung around like I belonged to someone. No one ever asked."

"Didn't any of the other ladies know?"

"Yeah, but I could get things they wanted from the ship's stores, being small and all. It weren't steal'n they didn't give the women enough to eat to stay healthy."

He didn't want her approval. He'd suffered so much for a child. "Your mother must have been a special lady to have raised such a fine son, she would be proud of you, David."

When he turned towards her, Jolene wrapped him in her embrace to comfort the tears. "Hush now and rest David, you have a home now."

The first cry of alarm came close to dawn. Jolene looked at David trying not to show him how afraid she truly felt.

Flint hadn't been by to check on them for some time, and she worried where he might be, praying he would stay put.

David's whisper was hardly audible. "I see something moving in the mist by the tress."

Jolene moved closer to the boy, preparing she knew to shield him if necessary.

"Don't shoot unless you are sure it's..." But she never had a chance to finish.

They came from everywhere with the hideous war cries shattering the silence. Guns sounded from all around them. Gripping David's arm they both held back from shooting, remembering Flint's warning not to until they were close. Having only six guns they couldn't afford to waste any bullets. The time it took to reload became all too precious.

"They're getting pretty close Jolene." The boy's fear made him use her name. Her own fright wasn't any better.

"We will wait like Flint said...make every shot count David."

"Tell me when."

The question of killing another human being came, but was quickly dismissed over the screams she could hear down the wagon line.

When her first shot came she didn't wait to see if the man fell. Picking up the next weapon she took aim on the next charging figure. David started reloading, leaving her to shoot the weapons he replaced in her outstretched hand. The need to shoot at the mass of attacking savages quickly used up all the loaded guns before David's efforts could reload.

Joining him Jolene finished one.

"Look out!"

Turning with the pistol in hand she fired point-blank into the large body trying to tear away the blockade they hid behind. His vicious scream stunned her, not sure if it came from pain or anger. Watching him fall back to the ground before their makeshift fort snapped her out of the shock. Seeing more coming left no time for fright.

How long they kept coming she couldn't remember. All she saw was there wasn't anyone charging them to fire at. She refused to see all the bodies sprawled out before their wagon.

"David?"

"Is it over?"

"I think so, for now." They worked to reload all the guns before staring at each other. Holding her arms out to him he moved into her embrace. Rocking him she tried to still his sobs, fighting to keep her own buried.

"Jolene!"

Flint's call made the relief bubble up inside her. "Here Flint, we're alright."

Crawling out of the path he cleared for them, he lifted her up in his arms before she could get off her knees. "Oh my Darlin'!" He held her tight over the emotion choking them. "Come here boy."

Flint lifted David up into their circle. "You did real good David, I'm proud of you."

"Mrs. Flint!"

They all turned to the frantic cry as one of the ladies rushed into the area.

"Please, you must help us, there are so many wounded."

Flint took charge. "We'll take them all to McKean's camp, it's the most protected. I'll get the men together."

Turning to Jolene, "Are you sure you are alright?"

"I'll be fine Flint, you go on. I'll get together what we need."

Seeing him leave again was almost as bad as the battle still fresh in her memory.

"Dear God, so many!"

Turning, Jolene saw the shock on Mrs. Clark's stricken face over the bodies before the wagon. "Anna?"

"Oh, I'm sorry Mrs. Flint, it's just, well I can't understand."

"What?"

"It's nothing, what do I know."

"Mrs. Clark?" Jolene's arm came about her waist to ward off the feelings coming over her.

But the lady just shook her head in sympathy and started walking away.

After gathering up her medical supplies, David and Jolene followed. Jolene gave orders to each wagon over what to bring to McKean's for the wounded. As they walked through camp her steps began to slow. David's hand slipped into hers. Stopping, Jolene turned back to survey the destruction as if to confirm what she now saw for herself. Only one or two dead braves lay scattered about in front of each wagon. Their own camp had been littered with the evidence of the assault.

When David's hand tugged on her skirt, she looked down at him. Their gazes met in understanding. "It's over."

Was it? Was Awasos here? Lurking within the forest, waiting? Had he deliberately launched his men in force against her?

CHAPTER 18
Cold Facts

The ill thoughts didn't leave Jolene as she tended the wounded men. Most of the injuries were not critical, and she soon tended them. Only one man's condition frightened her, older than the majority and a loner. He'd taken an arrow in his chest and nothing she tried stopped the heavy bleeding.

When McKean approached her she left Mr. Brent to get more bandages, Jolene didn't have the strength left to keep up any front.

"Well? Will he make it?"

Shaking her head, "I don't think so."

"You've done all you could and we're grateful Mrs. Flint."

Mr. Brent died shortly after their conversation.

Jolene kept busy with the minor cuts left to care for.

Seeing to everyone, she settled the more serious about McKean's blockade. Having seen nothing of Flint, she sought out McKean.

"Where is Flint?"

"He's off with some of the men, clearing away the dead."

She wanted to go back to the wagon, but was unsure what to do without Flint. Jolene refused to admit that her hesitation had anything to do with Awasos.

Walking away from McKean, she fought with the turmoil inside. The unsettling sight coming back to her, made her halt. "McKean?"

"Yes Mrs. Flint...Damn!"

The man moved up before her, breaking her mesmerized gaze. Approaching them under a flag of truce were three French Officers.

Backing away from the men gathering around McKean, Jolene felt her panic rise.

Searching for David she called him to her. "David find Flint, hurry!"

Moving away from the men Jolene wished Flint would come.

He arrived, running into camp with the urgency David must have conveyed. She wanted so to run to him.

Seeing how shaken Jolene looked and the cause, "David go to her and keep her by the wagon."

"Yes sir. It's the Indians, she's scared of, the way they came at us more than the others."

Roughing the boy's hair. "I know son, now go on and stay with her."

Flint cursed the reason that kept him from being at his wife's side. Seeing what he'd failed to at first in their camp, he could imagine how Jolene felt.

That bastard tried to get her. Awasos directed his well planned attack right at their wagon. Pinning Flint down here with McKean, Flint hadn't been able to reach Jolene. Flint still couldn't believe she'd been able to keep them from overtaking her. The bodies he'd carted away from before the wagon told him what neither of them wanted to admit.

The men parted for Flint to join McKean, who was out front talking to the officers. Flint scanned the area beyond them, but if that bastard was out there he wouldn't be seen.

"Flint, this is Captain Le Beck. He and his men have come to talk."

Grinding his teeth down to keep his mounting anger in check, Flint let McKean continue.

"I've explained to the captain why we are here."

"Oui monsieur, it is unfortunate we were not aware of your purpose before."

"You seem to feel differently now Captain Le Beck."

"Why of course. Monsieur McKean has accepted our apology for the misunderstanding of our overzealous companions."

"You mean your savages, Captain?" Flint's attack on the man made McKean fidget.

"It is unfortunate that they acted before we could meet with you. I assure you they will be punished for their indiscretion."

Flint wanted to laugh at the man's excuse. McKean stepped in preventing him from moving toward the man.

"Flint, the captain explained the error and offered us safe conduct to the territory."

"And who's going to guard us? The Iroquois?"

The captain's brow shot up. "No monsieur, my own troops will escort you the rest of the way."

McKean, the blind fool. Nothing Flint might say could change what would be coming. Leaving them, Flint went to Jolene.

"Come on."

"Flint, what's happening?"

"The fool man is swallowing all that fancy Frenchman spits out."

Walking beside him Jolene tried to look back at McKean, but instead met the tall officer's gaze and his smile of acknowledgment for her.

Flint's hand at her elbow drew Jolene's attention away.

Thankfully, there wasn't any evidence left at their camp for what happened that morning. Flint sent David to start the fire.

Jolene looked at Allen. He was a walking storm. "You want to tell me?"

His hands held her arms. "Ah Darlin' I just don't trust them. McKean has accepted the French captain's offer for an escort to the territory."

"But Flint, how could he after what's happened?"

She could sense that he refused to discuss it any further.

That afternoon McKean tried to talk with Flint. Jolene watched them arguing out of hearing range. Flint stalked back towards her, McKean following him.

"Flint?" McKean sounded nervous.

"No!"

McKean turned towards Jolene. "Maybe you can talk some sense into him, if so I'll see you both for dinner."

Flint's arm came about her shoulders as they watched him huff back through the wagons.

"David started the fire and I've got the beans on, we'll eat soon."

Neither of them spoke about McKean's outburst. Jolene figured out the dinner included the French officers.

Flint grew very moody during the evening meal. Jolene sent David off to bed, the boy practically fell asleep chewing.

In the distance they could hear the revelry coming from McKean's camp.

"Go on to bed, Jolene."

"Are you coming?"

Pulling her into his arms, "Not right away, though it's not for wanting not to."

She pressed her cheek against his chest. "You think he's out there don't you?" She felt him stiffen.

"I need to find out. We can't leave the train if he is."

Jolene didn't sleep, listening in the darkness she heard when Flint snuck off into the night.

Sitting in the wagon she kept the pistol across her lap and waited for him to return.

Flint didn't return until the morning sky began to lighten.

They broke camp in strained silence. Chancing a look at him walking beside her as the wagon moved out, Jolene knew the answer he wouldn't speak of... Awasos was still out there.

Throughout the morning Flint never left her side, refusing to answer McKean's hail to join him and the French captain at the front. Her searching gaze found his, silently telling her he wouldn't leave her side.

The rare treat of having Flint's company for the day would have been glorious if not for the horrible threat behind his presence. He told her they would stay with the wagons. She knew Awasos could be the only reason that would make Flint stay with McKean.

Jolene envied David's lack of awareness. The boy was in his glory having Flint to himself. He pestered Flint with so many questions she knew he must have been saving them up. Flint found his patient nature for the boy and never once gave any indication of the trouble she caught when their eyes met. They both realized that to leave would mean disaster.

More than half the men found their way to Flint's side during the day's trek. All were concerned over what their eyes could see. Most were as leery as Flint over the escort. Flint told them to be on guard for what might be traveling along with them in the woods. These men came along way from the ones that left Fort Pratt. Jolene wondered how McKean would take their new-found strength and independence when he finally confronted it. The time would come, sooner than the man realized if his new friendship turned false.

She prayed McKean's papers honestly made Captain Le Beck change his intent, and he was truly giving them the escort for the right reasons. For now, she felt relieved to have Flint near to take away her fears.

CHAPTER 19
Elizabeth

"She's dead, Jolene!"

"Charlotte!"

The woman's eyes met Jolene's in sympathy before stating what neither of them wanted to see.

"You can't do any more, Jolene."

A cry came from the small bundle Jolene placed beside the unmoving body of the baby girl's mother. She wiped the tears falling down her cheek. Charlotte spoke only the truth, the woman called Elizabeth was gone. They struggled these last hours to save mother and child, during the pain riddled birth. But only the infant survived. Elizabeth hemorrhaged and Jolene could only curse the lack of her knowledge and facilities to help the woman.

Picking up the tiny baby Jolene left the wagon when Charlotte told her to go.

Flint lifted her down before the silent crowd that gathered about the Brown camp.

She looked up at the strong man that gave her so much strength. He saw her answer and the pain for the death neither of them could prevent.

Holding the child Jolene walked over to Mr. Brown. The man's face bore a cold mask against what she felt he already knew. The silencing of his wife's screams already told everyone what happened. Flint stood beside her and she felt so grateful for his support.

"Mr. Brown, I'm sorry. But your daughter is healthy and should do just fine."

The man's eyes rose, shocking Jolene with their cold vehemence. Flint must have felt it too, for his arm came about Jolene's shoulders.

"Taint my child that ungrateful bitch died for. Too bad you didn't let the brat die too."

Her head shook in denial. "Mr. Brown!"

"Nay woman, you keep it or let it die, it matters little either way to me. I won't waste my time any longer on her bastard."

The angry man stalked off, pushing his way past the others. Flint kept her from following.

"But the baby? What about this little girl?" Jolene scanned the crowd as if seeking an answer, but all of them just looked sorry for what just happened.

Her lips pressed tight to stop their trembling.

Flint wanted to ease the pain he witnessed in his wife. No one knew better than him how hard she'd tried to save the woman and what it cost her. When her hand went protectively about the small head his own words came back to laugh at him...*every stray!*

He knew exactly what that satin gaze would ask when she sought him out.

"Darlin'?" *Damn it Jolene!* Flint couldn't deny her any more than he could the feelings he held for this special woman.

"I can't just leave her, Flint."

Shaking his head, he leaned back and stared at the night sky. "No, I don't suppose we can. Come on, let's get her home."

Flint took the baby from her arms, holding it as if he had experience with such a wee thing, making Jolene's brow arch in question.

"Four brothers and three sisters didn't allow for one to be unaware of babes."

Jolene's fingers pressed through his fine hand. "Do you think she will accept the oxen's milk?"

"When she's hungry enough, she'll stop arguing."

That night was the longest she remembered. Flint fixed up a leather nipple over the bottle David finally secured from one of the other camps. Jolene's insistence that it all be sterilized in boiling water before the milk touched it, exasperated both males walking about to sooth the crying baby.

When she fell silent sucking hard on the delayed nourishment, both of them looked at her as if she'd created a big mistake.

Little Beth showed one hellish temper for being so tiny and a demanding voice that let everyone know exactly what she wanted.

The last days on the trail found their time devoted to the new member of their fast growing...family.

Though Flint grumbled over the lack of sleep, he would be the first to answer the little cherub's cries. Jolene thought she couldn't love this man any more than she did, but she found her heart overflowing for what time gave to her.

Mr. Brown left the group that night, without a word to anyone. Charlotte told Jolene that the couple never stopped fighting since the first night. More often than not, poor Elizabeth bore the evidence of their violent arguments.

Gifts for the baby came from all direction, clothes, material for more and diapers. Jolene almost felt their conscience made them come forth and then scolded her nasty thoughts. But no one offered to take the baby. And after the first night she knew she wouldn't have given her up. Watching how Flint and David took to their little girl, anyone that tried to take her would have to fight these two to get to her.

Flint continued to stay with them during the last of their journey to McKean's territory. The French came with their tracker. Jolene knew Flint went out every night to see if Awasos still followed. She never asked and almost forgot about the threat stalking them because of the baby's demand on her time. It wasn't until Flint's solemn mood became too obvious to ignore that she approached him after supper.

Sitting down beside him, she snuggled into the shoulder he offered.

"She's gone down early tonight."

Jolene smiled into the fire. "Beth is getting into a routine. Did you notice how chubby she is getting?"

"She's a regular glutton for Daisy's milk."

"Will the ox have enough milk when her calf is born?"

"I think she'll put out for both babies."

Holding onto his arms wrapped about her waist, she forced the question out. "What's wrong Flint?"

He nuzzled her hair. It was getting longer, where he could wrap his fingers into the silky waves. Sighing, he didn't do a very good job of hiding his thoughts from her. "He's gone, moved out his men day before last."

Jolene's fingers tightened on Flint's arm. Awasos was gone! "Then we can leave?"

When he didn't answer, she started to turn, but he held her fast against him.

"Flint?"

"We'd never get through the mountains in time to avoid the snows."

She realized he was right, already there'd been a light frost, but they were still high.

"McKean has offered to increase my share to a thousand acres if we stay."

This time she didn't let him stop her from turning to see him. Cupping his face, she saw the deep line of worry that became a part of him of late.

"Allen, I'll go wherever you decide. It doesn't matter where or what we do."

He eased her across his lap. "I know Darlin'. I guess I've been doing a lot of thinking over the things you've told me."

They talked of so many things these last weeks, Jolene told him everything she could remember about things that would happen in his future.

His fingers absently traced her lips. "This is going to be a busy country pretty soon and it doesn't seem to matter much where we might be living. I don't see how a person can avoid being caught up in it."

"Allen, I didn't mean to upset you."

He smiled down at her. "You didn't, it's not every man that has his own spy into the future. I guess I've just been arguing with myself over how, or if, I should take advantage of the gift of foresight."

She felt his body relax. So many reasons for his mood crossed her mind, she never thought of this one. "You know we can't change what will come."

"No, I don't think knowing will stop anything. But it does make me aware of what to look out for."

"Like what Allen?"

"McKean has come out further than anyone else, even the French. They were eager to give him the grant because their own settlers wouldn't venture this far."

"So?"

"So, my lovely time traveler, it makes senses to settle out here. You said the Colonies would gain possession of Louisiana by 1803. Most of the fighting should be finished and the concentration will be to move farther west. You must tell me again about the west and what's out there."

"Allen Flint!"

He laughed at her. "We really should see, don't you think?"

Such an adventurer! "No doubt, now come on and tell me what else you have decided."

"I thought we'd take the old man up on his offer. I choose the land that runs along the river."

"Prime property."

"My guess exactly. How's a trading post sound Mrs. Flint?"

"We'll need a dock for the boats."

"I think you may be ahead of yourself, maybe our children will need a dock. No doubt a nice beach will do for now for the flat boats I suspect will be coming down river, in time."

"Ah, but have you forgotten about the shipping that will come up river? I have it on good authority that New Orleans will be a major world shipping port."

Flint tickled her, but just as quickly turned serious again.

"Jolene, we mustn't move too fast."

"McKean?"

"Him, but more the French. They may regret giving up the land if it begins to look too appealing."

"Then we must make sure we are accepted in their eyes."

He studied that mischievous light in her alluring eyes. "Did your grandfather also teach you to be a schemer?"

"No, just cautious and to watch my back."

"Smart man."

"Allen, are you sure you want to do this? We can go back."

"I doubt that Massachusetts will be any better than here. My brother can lease out the land for me. We don't have to make any decisions on it right away."

"Are all your brothers and sisters here?"

"No, only two, Kevin is the landowner."

"And the other?"

"Josh, now he would no doubt interest you more. He is a shipper and I might add, very successful. He owns many ships that are always looking for new ports."

Jolene's laughter drew his. "Mr. Flint you are a sly one."

"I have to be to keep up with my growing family."

Jolene's hand came up and cupped his jaw. "Do you mind so terribly, Allen?"

"Mind? No. Surprised, yes. Delighted to have two very healthy and pleasing children? Definitely, and such a wife that accepts us all with love." His arm came around her shoulders and gently pulled her to his side. "I'd say Mrs. Flint that my life has changed in the most rewarding way."

"As my own, dear husband. I do love you so much Allen."

Flint's kiss held a hunger for this woman, one he felt would never be satisfied. He gloried in her passion and the fire she reached out to him with, for she touched his soul. Jolene was heaven and earth, all softness and wild boldness that drove him mad with the desire to possess her.

Lifting her up in his arms he carried her over to the wagon and laid her inside the confines of the tent they'd erected beneath the wagon. Both of their eyes raised at little Beth's small whimper, coming from inside the wagon where the children now slept.

Jolene smothered her laughter against his shoulder as Flint blew out his breath when the baby didn't start fussing. Pulling him down over her, they hastened to shed their clothes that kept them apart.

She ran her hands over his fine chest and rained tiny kisses over the warm golden flesh. His muscles rippled in awareness under her ardent caresses, so much man, "Oh what you do to me Allen."

That familiar fire in the core of her womb blazed to life for the want of his touch. Her fingers closed over the bold, solid length, and she drew him into her wet folds.

"Oh wife, you are so beautiful, I want to bury myself inside you Jolene and never leave you." His tongue traced the open smile on her lips, "you taste like honey and warm life that makes me hungry for you."

"Take me Allen, oh please...now."

He drove into her, and she tightened around the power of Flint, for she too wanted to hold him inside, keep him there...forever! And when he entered and went deeper, touching the heart of her sexual core, Jolene cried her love for him in loving whispers, begging him to go deeper, wanting the union only this man could deliver.

The force of his driving suddenly worried Flint as his hands held her tiny hips. But when he would have slowed the passionate assault, Jolene lunged up and took him in. She became liquid fire, pure ecstasy, and he knew no one would ever be as precious to him as this woman, his wife. "I love you so much my Darlin'..."

"I'm yours Allen, only you hold my love."

Allen felt the surge of power she always filled him with, and he buried himself to the hilt. She moved in a sensual dance that made him crazy and ignited all his senses. His tongue toyed with her breast before latching on to the sensitive teat and Allen sucked deep, drawing in the very essence of this beautiful woman. And when she groaned in wanton hunger for more, Allen caught the other and shared the pleasure, nipping and tickling her teat until she went crazy from the tender caressing. When she pushed up to take him, Allen plunged into her with a fury he'd not reached with Jolene before.

Her legs came up and wrapped about his waist telling him in no uncertain terms that this was right. What they shared in their sexual bliss is what she wanted as much as he did and it would never be enough.

When he pulled his throbbing length out of her slick folds Jolene cried in protest, but when he lifted her hips and his mouth closed over the sweet folds of her pussy Jolene went silent. She watched as he slowly licked the essence of their joined sex and he watched her reaction when his tongue slid into the hot crevice he'd left wanting. Allen's tongue drove into the honeyed folds of her pussy and Jolene thought she would go mad, the sensations of feeling his tongue inside her became more erotic than anything he ever did to her. "Oh my...Allen!"

"Let it happen, my Darlin', let me love you like I've wanted to for so long."

She couldn't answer for her breaths were coming in quick short gasps as he tortured her clit with the tip of his tongue. When his lips closed over that nub of pure pleasure her whole body rocked in his hold, yet he wouldn't release her, and he sucked and licked the hot sexual juices that flowed from her until she cried beneath his tender lovemaking. And when Jolene felt her insides start to tighten she knew she was going to explode. "Allen please, love, please put it back inside, I need to feel you, I need your power inside me, driving to my very core...oh Allen, now, please Allen..."

He pulled her into his lap and held her up, just over the tip of his magnificent rod. She could feel it jumping beneath her, and he moved her over the pulsing head. She tried to take him in, but Allen held her still. "Feel it Jolene, because it has never wanted any woman before like this, and it will never touch any woman's sex but yours...wife!"

And with that mortal vow he pulled her hot spice over the shaft of his empowered shaft and Jolene's cry of ecstasy was silenced by the devouring lips of the man that just took her to the palace of passion. And when he lay back he brought her with him, never separating their joining, and he held her above him and elevated her over and up the full length before easing her back down the solid shaft of his volatile erection. It only took a couple of rocking thrill rides for Jolene to join in and take over the full power of their joining.

Her hips moved in a dance as natural as when the wind flowed through the trees, and she smiled over the power he gave her over him. His hands were still on her hips, she knew he would catch her if she started to fall. Her own hands gripped his forearms and with their support she moved over him in taunting slowness, for now it was her turn to charm this man. The smile he returned to her coy stare said he knew exactly what she held in store for him.

"Jolene..."

"Hush, Allen, just enjoy the moment, my love."

With the last word Jolene let the full weight of her body plunge down over the top of him and in a rush she took the full force of his length inside. Then she let the warm fluids flow around his length as she held him inside. "I want to do that again."

Before he could answer she rose up and dropped over him. Their mutual groans of satisfaction flowed through the tent. He raised his knees up to give her more leverage and she laughed as she let herself love this gorgeous man!

Their joining went fast and furious, and they drove into each other as if they were starved to feel, hungry to reach passion's pinnacle that only two people in love can ever achieve.

The very touch of his rough palms circling her nipples sent Jolene over the edge and she exploded around him and held on to him with such a force Allen moaned. His arms pulled her against his chest and he held on to her as he rolled her beneath him. He drove deeper, pushing into her swollen spice until he felt himself go crazy, and in an awesome surge he spread his seed into the depths of her womb. Pushing and driving ever deeper, holding himself into her pulsing sweetness, Flint vowed, "My child this time Jolene, we need our own."

"Yes, oh yes Allen, I want your baby!"

He kissed her trembling lips as their tremors gentled, yet neither wanted to let go.

Flint pulled the covers over them as he eased her into his side. He kissed the top of her head and she snuggled closer. His embrace tightened, praying he could keep her safe and beside him forever.

CHAPTER 20
Alliances

"More stew, Captain?"

"Madam, I cannot thank you enough for inviting me, yes please." The man turned to Flint. "Your wife is a wonderful cook, Monsieur Flint."

"She is, though I'd say you would find any fare other than McKean's enjoyable."

Jolene shot Flint a scolding glare over the man's laughter.

Handing the captain another bowl, Jolene went over and picked up little Beth for her evening bottle.

"She is a beautiful little girl. It is rare to find people willing to take in another's child in these times."

So McKean's tongue hadn't slowed any. Flint took away Jolene's need to answer.

"They are both ours now."

"Oui, yes, I can see the truth."

Jolene blushed over the man's intense gaze that remained on her. Caption Le Beck wasn't attractive as much as he appeared impressive. Taller than Flint, he possessed a thin frame, but his body coiled tight like a spring, making her wonder if he ever relaxed. His coal-black hair seemed to intensify the sharp angles of his face. Stiff, yes, like his fine military uniform.

"I am relieved that our differences have been settled Monsieur Flint."

"Not settled Captain, only gone for the time being."

The man's eyes sharpened like a blade over Flint's meaning. "I regret their presence lingered so long, but the savage was not an easy man to convince to leave."

Flint's gaze caught Jolene's in warning. He only told her it would be best to keep Awasos out of their dealings with this man.

"You should not worry any longer, they will not return and all the other tribes in the territory are friendly enough to our settlers."

Neither of them missed the emphasis the Captain put on 'our'. Jolene needed to bite her lip not to voice her hatred for what these men would do to innocent people in the colonies.

Inviting the captain to dinner had been her idea, she hoped it would be the beginning of a satisfying alliance for their future in this territory. Above all else she, like Flint, needed to think of their future among these people. Voicing their opinions weren't to be allowed to happen.

"Captain, are you and your men stationed near our new settlement?"

"Oui Madam, near enough to watch over you so no harm will come from outsiders."

Jolene decided it best to let him believe her a helpless female, it became an amenable lie. "Do you think there will be any trouble?"

"No, no, but we must take precautions, this is a wilderness."

She left the men to discuss the work ahead. They would reach McKean's grant in about a week.

Jolene put little Beth and David down for the night. Kissing them both before leaving the wagon David called to her.

"Did he mean what he said to the captain?"

Her gaze went over to Flint. "Yes David, he meant every word. You and Beth are our children now."

"Then I can call you mother?"

"If you want." She smiled and smoothed his hair down. "Goodnight David."

"Mother...I like that."

"So do I, sweet dreams son."

She busied herself with clearing up the dishes. The captain was asking Flint if he would track for him once he got his family settled in. Jolene held her breath over Flint's answer.

"It would depend on the area and purpose."

"You are a cautious man."

"It has kept me alive, Captain."

Flint defused the man's wariness, but Jolene felt that the captain sensed Flint's true nature. Some things would just have to be accepted on both sides.

The week sped by with everyone getting more anxious. Captain Le Beck became a nightly visitor at their evening meal and Jolene actually felt Flint liked the man. She stayed in the background, remaining a little leery of the man's apt attention concerning her. He never stepped beyond the strict decorum of gentleman, she planned on giving him no reason to change.

When the captain asked Flint to accompany him the next morning, to go on ahead to the land tract, she tried desperately not to show what it did to her. Every night Flint snuck off when he thought her to be asleep, she knew he did so to confirm that Awasos didn't return. She felt Flint's gaze burning into her, asking for her answer.

Jolene called on all the courage left to her. She turned and gave him a nod of consent, telling herself it would be foolish to feel so scared.

Flint moved their wagon up by McKean's that next morning. The captain made a point of letting her see him order his men to guard Mrs. Flint until they returned. Watching them ride off Jolene couldn't shake the terrible thought that the captain knew the reason for Flint's concern. "But that's silly."

"What is mother?"

"Me, David, just your mommy."

"You are not silly, you are pretty."

"Thank you." Settling the squirming Bess into the halter Flint made for her to carry the baby in, so her arms would be free, Jolene pushed her worry aside. "We'd best catch up with Mr. McKean."

"On devil!" David eased the great brown ox out, his protesting bellow earned the boy's reprimand. "Only two more days you lazy cow."

She swore the big eyes rolled up at the boy, making them both burst out in laughter. Little Bess' arms and legs kicked as she gurgled happily along with them.

The day felt as if it would never end, reminding her of another time Flint left them. She'd not rest until they caught up to them tomorrow.

They ate dinner with McKean and the captain's officers. Conversation proved trying as the men's English was poor. Jolene's one year of high school French only went so far and each laughed at the other's attempt to communicate. They were all about her age, and she noted the difference in them compared to their strict captain. Le Beck appeared to be in his mid thirties, she managed to ask the lieutenant about Captain Le Beck's past command.

McKean helped translate the boy's words. Their Captain Le Beck had been in the Spanish conflicts and also held the claim as a direct descendant of King Louis XIV. The news didn't surprise her, the man had a way about him that spoke of high breeding. She could easily picture him in court of the King's palace. Or walking in full uniform down the streets of Paris. In fact he didn't fit the wilderness he now commanded in, making her wonder how he came to be here at all.

That night Bess fussed terribly. Jolene blamed herself, suspecting that the baby picked up on her worry. Walking about the dimly lit camp, she tried to comfort the child, all the while telling herself everything would be fine. Yet every night noise left her jumpier than the last. Looking about her, not even seeing the guards in French uniforms could settle her nerves. If it wasn't for the children she knew she would have left the camp to find Flint!

Everyone maintained high spirits throughout the day. Jolene tried to appear as elated as her friends.

Reaching the start of what McKean claimed as the grant, the cloth ties about the trees could only have been put there by Flint and the Captain. A loud cheer went racing through the wagons.

With each step her eyes searched for a sign of Flint. The land tapered down, out of the hills into the flat expanse that she felt would eventually lead to the river. Her heart raced when he rode out of the tree line.

"David, watch Bess."

Jolene's feet hastened their pace. Picking up the long folds of her skirt she gave into their freedom to race towards him.

God, but she was a sight!

Racing down the hill the sun made her hair glow a bright red as it flew out behind her. Jumping down from his horse in time, Flint caught her as she jumped into his outstretched arms. Swinging her about, she held his face in her hands and his lips to her own.

When she finally began to relax, he gently set her down on her feet. "Oh Darlin', I should leave more often."

"Don't you dare Allen Flint, don't you dare."

He recaptured her swollen lips, staking his own claim over what he'd missed.

The Captain rode up checking his mount, making him pace in a tight circle. Tipping his hat to her, "Madam, you are lovelier than I remember. I envy not having a lady such as yourself awaiting my return."

"I'll join you in a few minutes, Captain."

"Take your time, I would." The man dug his heels in sending the horse racing away.

"Rather forward, isn't he?"

Flint looked down at her. "There is much to that man, Jolene, be careful around him."

"I already am."

"I know, Darlin', just don't let his charm fool you."

"There is only one man that has ever charmed me."

His gaze held her own in playful warning. "It had best be me, my Darlin', or I may have to kill the upstart."

The night turned into a grand celebration. Everyone danced and sang and talked of the future. They left the party early because of the children, but Jolene couldn't keep her smile hidden over Flint's excuse.

They talked of the land he'd finally seen. She loved how he got excited over telling her about it and his ideas on how they'd make it productive. He couldn't tell her where he planned to build their house, only telling her she'd know when she saw it.

McKean decided it would be best for all to separate as they came within their section, so each family could survey their plot and make plans for building their homestead. All would meet up at the site of the proposed stockade in three weeks time. For everyone's safety the Captain promised to use his men to help erect the fort. Then they all would come to do what might be needed to finish the blockade.

To Jolene's pleasant surprise the Stokes were to be their closest neighbors. Flint set her straight, telling her that close meant a good two mile walk. After the distance they'd come it seemed a small bit of land.

Even from the distance she could see the place Flint must have chosen for the house. Atop a slight rise stood three large trees, they were spread perfectly apart, she could picture a house right between them.

"How is the vision, Darlin'?"

"Working very well, tell me, how do we start?"

"One large structure with a loft at first."

"It sounds wonderful. Will it take long?"

Looking at her hopeful gaze, Flint didn't think tomorrow would be soon enough, telling her it might be weeks seemed too painful. "Why, we'll work until it is up."

David chimed in, "I can use an ax."

"Really son, well, I believe I have one you can use and if Bess were a little bigger I'd make her one too."

"Girls can't swing an ax."

The old Jolene's rankles came alive. "Oh really, young man."

Flint just laughed and tossed David's hair. "I think your mother has some very different ideas on what a woman can do. I'd listen if you want peace in this new home of ours."

They didn't waste a minute of the day.

Flint walked out the length and width of the base plan, staking it off with David's help. Jolene went about setting up their new temporary camp with more permanence than the trail allowed.

Bess was just beginning to roll around from her back to her stomach. It wouldn't be long before she began to crawl. Jolene mentally designed the playpen she would ask Flint to make. That led to the thought of a high chair and crib, but she pushed them all aside, the first task was their home.

David went with Flint to the large stand of trees to mark off the ones they would begin cutting in the morning, while she started dinner. Her senses followed them until they entered the woods. It seemed every bit of her came alert to this new place. As she went about dinner she would stop every so often and mentally take note of the distance to the river that was a good five hundred feet from the knoll or to the other grove of trees to the north, beyond the meadow. She would explore it all the first chance she got. The rise they were settled in looked high enough to be out of danger should the river turn mean. A small creek ran around the knoll where the house would be, making it easy to draw water without a long haul. The ground around them showed dark and rich, with the meadow relatively clear to the tree line. It wouldn't be too difficult to plant this spring.

She wished they weren't looking at winter coming on. There were enough supplies, but she needed to try and find some wild nuts and other roots, maybe even some fresh fruit, before it got too cold. If she could make a net she could catch fish and smoke some for the winter.

It proved hard getting everyone to go to sleep that night, they all kept talking as they lay there under the stars about everything that would need to be done. When they finally started to say goodnight, it was Jolene that burst out laughing. She couldn't help it, visions of the Walton's flooded in on her as they each called out goodnight to the other. She would explain to Flint later, for David's sake she said she was just too happy to contain it.

Rising before first light she made breakfast to have it ready before anyone woke, including Beth. Feeding the baby, she let the men help themselves. Jolene decided to try and feed Beth milky porridge and the child took to it with gusto.

"A glutton, I told you she was."

"Well at least she won't miss Daisy's milk if the calf takes it all." Looking over at the oxen. "She's awful big. When do you think she will have it?"

"Could be any time now. At least old Rose isn't carrying. I need a barn before they get a herd started. We will use Devil and Job as the team for the logs today."

"Won't the others run off?"

"Nah, we'll hobble them just to be safe, but I don't think the girls will leave the fellows." Flint gave her a wink that made her blush.

"I want to go look for roots and nuts while you are cutting."

"Only where I tell you. A falling tree can kill a man."

They all entered the woods following Flint. He pointed out where they would be working and showed her the area she could start in. Before she left them he made her take the pistol and his hunting knife. "You do remember how they work?"

"If you're serious, I'd be glad to show you."

He took her sarcasm to his heart playing as if she'd wounded him, while David practically rolled on the ground with laughter.

With a huff she started off, throwing them each a kiss over her shoulder. Juggling the baby, basket and gun wasn't going well. She finally stopped and slid the sheathed knife into her skirt waist. The pistol she placed in the basket. "There Bess, now we will do some serious looking. Keep your eyes open for a pecan tree."

The ringing of Flint's ax echoed through the tree tops. "Daddy's determined to chop down at least five this morning. What do you think, Bess, can he do it?"

"Maybe with help your husband can make it ten."

Stumbling back from the unexpected voice. "Captain!"

"Mon dieu, madam, I did not mean to startle you."

His eyes dropped to her hand clutching the knife's hilt. "Pardon, forgive me?"

Taking a steadying breath she tried to get a hold of her racing heart. "Next time monsieur, I suggest you call out or whistle before approaching."

"Oui, I will remember."

Jolene decided it must be his eyes that bothered her. They were so piercing the way they seemed to go through her defenses. It made her nervous. "If you are serious about helping, I am sure Flint would be pleased."

His smile told her he'd seen more than what she cared for. "Oui, I will join him, unless I can help you?"

"No thank you. I will be fine."

He left with a curt nod.

She watched him head towards the resounding ax. It wasn't long before there were two rings in measured beats.

The first tree sounded like thunder when it toppled. She smiled over their shouts of success. Her own elation was just as pleasing when she discovered a stand of apple trees. Gathering all the basket would hold she headed back to make a surprise for her working family...and one Captain.

Waving, she caught Flint's notice and told him she would be going back to camp.

Jolene spent the rest of the day preparing a large supper and making an apple-betty for the boys. The air filled with the luscious mouth-watering aroma.

She counted twelve massive logs being dragged up behind the team. Flint looked magnificent. His bronzed bare torso glistened under the noon sun. His lips were spread in a wide grin over their achievement. Their good nature bantering came bounding into camp.

"My, my David but something sure smells good. I think Jolene found a surprise out in the woods."

"Go and wash."

"Ah, but I'm starving."

"Then you will get clean faster."

Flint pushed David forward, stopping to kiss her brow as he passed. "Apple-betty is my favorite, among some other sweet things."

"Go on and wash up." She could feel the blush creeping up her neck. Enraptured by his teasing she forgot about their guest. Jolene's cheeks blazed when she found him watching their exchange. The man's shirt was open to his waist. Unwanted, her gaze fell upon the tight expanse of capable muscles.

Flustered she quickly brought her eyes up only to have them meet his knowing ones. Nodding to her he followed the others to the creek.

Jolene mumbled under her breath, "Damn him, if he wasn't such a help I'd tell him to leave."

Jolene refused to let her ill mood spoil the day's pleasure. The supper by all counts proved a success. The apple-betty was completely gone after the men and David insisted on seconds.

Putting the dishes to soak Jolene rushed to clean up, wanting to go back to the woods for more apples.

Flint and the Captain started driving spikes into the logs to split them. Tomorrow Jolene reminded herself to start testing a clay mixture for chinking between the logs. Having helped her grandfather, she hoped she remembered the technique.

There just wasn't enough time for all the discoveries that afternoon. With David's help they gathered all the apples they could carry. To their pleasure they found peach and pecan trees, marking the trail for their return tomorrow. Jolene felt exhausted just thinking of all the gathering to be done and the cooking to follow. Filling it all in with the demands of the house wouldn't be easy, but somehow it would all get done.

To her dismay the Captain remained. She tried to be pleased, knowing how much Flint could accomplish with the man's help. But Jolene kept her distance.

"**I** will return in time to help raise the roof."

Flint's grip locked on the man's forearm. "Your help won't be forgotten."

The Captain's broad smile came unbidden. "These last days have been a welcomed change, I thank you."

Watching the man mount Flint noted the control Paul Le Beck used not to let his gaze drift to Jolene. Keeping his own composure wasn't easy.

"Five days should see the walls in place, Oui?"

"Yes, we'll expect you then."

Nodding, the man released his hold on the horse, sending clumps of dirt flying out behind their leave.

"He was a good help."

He'd felt her behind him before her guarded statement of the fact. "Yes, gave us at least a two week lead. I've only the roof beams left to cut." Damn! He didn't need to defend Paul to her. The man's help was all that had kept her contempt in check these last six days. The fact Flint found he could actually like and respect the man set hard. The reason he shouldn't, kept him on constant guard. Unfortunately, Jolene's instincts were razor sharp concerning Paul Le Beck.

Flint hoped the inner control Paul, so far exhibited around his wife, didn't falter.

Her arms encircled his waist from behind, taking away the darkness in his eyes.

"It's alright Flint."

Was it? He couldn't help but wonder. Was he being a fool to chance the man's attraction for his wife? Flint couldn't help feeling his own tolerance over the man's continued presence wasn't anything more than selfishness on his part.

"When it isn't Darlin' you let me know."

Jolene rested her cheek against the tense muscles of his back. His statement didn't need any answer, Flint would know without words if the lines were crossed by Captain Le Beck. As long as Flint stayed near, Jolene basked in his protective circle. She refused to think of the ill feelings that might come when he must leave them alone.

CHAPTER 21
Old Fears

Jolene walked through the doorway, turning in awe over Flint's accomplishments.

Hugging Beth, "Isn't it grand! Daddy is a wonder."

Begrudgingly, she said a silent thank you to Captain Le Beck. Having the main structure's logs cut Flint had been able to concentrate on setting the walls.

Her gaze went up to the open roof that remained to be finished. Today would be the sixth day since Le Beck left and promised to return. Flint didn't say anything about the man's tardiness, but Jolene felt his concern. Her own instincts told her something must have happened to keep him away.

Absently scanning the vast tree line about the knoll, Jolene scolded her worried thoughts. "Probably just military business... "Come on Bess, we have a lot to accomplish before Flint and David return."

Jolene set the baby into the swing Flint found the time to design out of a large oak limb. Jolene gathered up the mud mixture to begin chinking between the logs. Checking yesterday's efforts, she felt pleased to see the hardening clay took hold. "Thank you Grandpa."

How many times she'd spoken out to him in the last days she couldn't count. Shaking her head she never would have believed all the things he'd taught her would actually come into use. Thankfully, she remembered most of his teachings, though she did have to make a few tries on different projects before discovering the right method.

She gave a skeptical look at the fish now drying over the smoking fires. Her fingers absently rubbed together over the cuts left from the third attempt to weave together the catch basket. Taking Flint and David's teasing over the empty baskets she continually pulled in from the river, nearly defeated her. But she'd finally gotten the reed spacing right and her chin rose over the fillets now curing.

Two other racks stood ready for whatever meat Flint's hunt brought forth. The time waiting for Le Beck's arrival wouldn't be wasted. Though they were well south of any snow threat, the conflicts around them made them both cautious over the stores for the winter. If trouble did develop Jolene knew Flint wouldn't leave them alone, not even for food.

The mud felt cold when she dipped her hands into the bucket, but she soon dismissed the discomfort concentrating on shoving the gunk into every minute space. The back wall still needed to be completed and she hoped to finish it before they started on the roof. If Le Beck didn't come today she'd find a way to convince Flint to let her help. "He calls me stubborn."

Even after all they'd been through and knew her capable of, Flint refused to let her work on anything except the pulley to help raise the side logs in place. She laughed over the remembered argument and her foot stomping determination to get him to admit he needed her help to raise them. "I love you Allen, even if you are over protective."

God, but she did. Her heart overflowed with feelings for him. Every night she gave a prayer of thanks for the wonderful man in her life.

Hearing Beth's gurgles. "And you and David too, my whole beautiful family."

A secret smile came over her. "Have you guessed Flint? Is that why you have gotten so protective?"

Jolene closed her eyes. "Am I? Are we going to have a baby?"

Flint didn't say anything, but she knew how thrilled he would be. Not wanting to give either of them any false hopes, she'd remained silent over what she believed. She'd only missed one period, another week would give her the answer.

The musical sounds of the forest and Beth's contented chatter carried Jolene's thoughts through her task.

Climbing down off the ladder she looked at the empty bucket in disdain, she needed more mud from the riverbank. Checking on Beth, she gave the swing a gentle push to insure the baby remained asleep in her absence. Without taking Beth she could carry two buckets and make quick work of the gathering.

Wiping her hands on her jeans her eyes went to the noon sun. Changing into them after Flint and David left she didn't want to be caught in them by their return. Ruining one of her dresses went against Jolene's belief. Thoughts of Flint's reaction made her brow furrow, her disagreeable thoughts made her steps hasten towards the river.

Shoveling the last bit of mud into the bucket, an odd sound made Jolene's senses fire, stilling her movements. Her gaze moved cautiously around the cat and nine tails on the bank, before shifting up towards the house.

The tightness in her shoulders didn't ease over the peaceful scene that gave no evidence to her ill feeling. In slow deliberation she drew out the hunting knife from the leather sheath at her waist.

"Beth..."

Leaving the buckets Jolene gave into the surging fear. Dismissing her caution her legs found their speed up the slope. Her sharp glances searched frantically for the sensed danger. Heading toward the swing she saw Beth's sleeping lips absently sucking at the air. Her relief over the baby's well-being didn't take away the impending danger she still sensed.

Spinning about Jolene held the knife out before her, ready for whatever might spring out. She realized the forest went silent as if confirming the fear filling her heart. She could barely take the air into her lungs, knowing that at any second her world would explode!

When it happened Jolene felt as if her heart would burst out her chest it was beating so hard. "No!"

Her head swung right then left, but everywhere she looked another Indian appeared. She started to step back, but something made her stop and spin around. She shook her head at the figure standing spread legged before her, ready to take on whatever battle she wanted to give... "Awasos!"

She could feel her throat closing as the fear spread through her. Jolene moved to stand in front of the swing as if she could protect Beth from him. Would he hurt the baby? The ugly thought made her head shake at him. All those horrible facts of the bloody massacres she'd read in school flooded in on her.

Jolene could feel the men behind her, but she knew the only one she needed to watch... Awasos. He wouldn't want anyone else to take her down. Without thought Jolene turned the knife about in her hand, so she could have more control. He caught her movement and his eyes grew cold. She didn't want to look at him but grew more afraid to look away. Jolene pushed the memories away, knowing if she let them invade her thoughts she'd fail for sure.

Her eyes opened wide when his body moved, crouching lower, readying to attack. She moved the knife out in front of her. He didn't even look at it, only at her, as if he could hypnotize her with his concentration. She couldn't win, it was a harsh truth, but Jolene prayed... "I'll go, just don't hurt my baby, leave her here."

His eyes dropped to the knife she still held out at him. She let it drop out of her hand and his closed over her wrist, pulling her up against him. She pulled her gaze away and lowered her head in defeat. One of the others took hold of her other arm and pulled it behind her, Awasos said something, and she felt the rawhide being pulled tighter about her wrist as they tied her arms behind her. She didn't struggle, there was no sense in wasting her energy. But when Awasos moved towards the swing her body reeled at him, only to have her legs kicked out from under her sending her to the ground.

He looked at her, then the baby. She knew it must be only seconds, but it seemed like forever before he moved away from Beth and left her sleeping in the swing.

They were his hands that lifted her to her feet. His hold bit into her arm, she clenched her teeth not to show how much he hurt her. She didn't make a sound as he led her away, she did try to look back and see Beth, thankful that none of the other braves stayed back. Beth was safe.

Jolene's vision blurred for her heart felt truly crushed, she stumbled but Awasos's hold kept her up. She looked away from him, refusing to let him see how devastated she became. It took her sometime to control the tears threatening to fall, she refused to let them come, she wouldn't give him that satisfaction.

Their pace grew fast and they were nearly running, but Jolene's bound hands behind her back made it impossible to keep her balance. Awasos practically dragged her to make her keep up. When she fell again, her head swung up, and she glared at him, "If you would untie me I wouldn't fall."

The silent smirk he gave her was the only warning she received before he lifted her and swung her up and over his shoulder. The hard landing on her stomach across his shoulder knocked the air from her lungs. She hung over him head down and suffered branches scrapping her face until she gave up trying to hold herself away from his back, and she buried her face against his flesh to stop from being whipped by the branches.

She lost track of time and felt dizzier than any ride at the fair might cause. The blood really did rush to her head, she wondered why she never really believed that saying. When he finally slowed from the run to a fast walk he adjusted her weight, she could almost breathe again. She refused to feel where his hands were touching her, but it grew more difficult as one of them moved up between her thighs until he actually held her crotch.

Jolene bit her lip not to groan when he deliberately pressed his thumb into her clit as if he truly knew just where it rested beneath her jeans. The only thing she felt grateful for was that she wore the jeans and the material was thicker than a dress would have been.

How long they raced through the woods she couldn't say. But it was dusk before they finally stopped, and he pulled her from his shoulder. When he placed her on her feet Jolene couldn't feel a thing and would have fallen if he didn't catch her. Being held like a child in his arms became worse than having his thumb against her clit all day.

As if he just read her thoughts he brought his hand up to his face and took a deep sniff. She wished he'd stay silent for his first words to her made her feel sick. "Your scent is now a part of me. It will allow me to find you...anywhere, little scout."

She just stared at him as he set her on the ground and his laughter rang out. If her legs weren't asleep she would have tried to kick him, and he knew it and laughed harder at her frustrated growl.

Jolene didn't want to think about how sick she felt. As he moved away she let her head go back against the tree, she closed her eyes to fight off the dizziness that made want her throw up. But try as she did she lost the battle and barely managed not to fall face-first into her own vomit as she turned to empty her stomach.

The touch of hands holding her head up until she finished being sick were surprisingly gentle and Jolene couldn't believe that Awasos actually held her. He righted her up against the tree but didn't leave her. She held her breath as his hand came off her shoulder and lowered to cover her stomach. "You are with child. Who's child did you leave?"

"Mine."

His smile said he didn't believe her and Jolene felt too miserable to argue. "The mother died, so I took the baby."

He didn't say anything, just studied her for a few seconds before moving away and joining his men.

The night became an eternity for Jolene. Awasos only came back to her once to try and feed her some dried meat, but the smell only made her sick again. Her struggle to be rid of his hands on her only wasted her small store of energy. After she stopped being sick he left her alone and joined his men. She watched them around the campfire through half closed eyelids. She refused to fall asleep, but rested her forehead on her knees.

It came during one of the times her head laid on her knees that she heard a slight sound behind her. Hoping beyond hope, she didn't move and waited, holding her breath.

"Don't move, Darlin', I'm here." She could barely hear him, but when she felt his finger touch her palm her fingers closed around his touch. It was all she could do to breathe and not start crying.

"You just stay put, while Paul and I take care of things and get you back home."

She didn't move except to squeeze his finger in reply. "I'll cut your ties, but don't move...Darlin' Beth and David are fine, they miss their mommy, so when the fighting starts I want you to roll into these bushes behind you and stay down. Please do it my love, Paul has his soldiers here and they might not look before shooting."

Flint waited for her to squeeze his finger, he could see another shudder tear through her and prayed she wasn't hurt. After cutting the rawhide ties he moved silently away from her to join Paul for the attack on Awasos' group.

Everything happened so fast that Jolene's sobs caught in her throat as she rolled into the brush as Flint wanted her to. She didn't dare move, gunfire kept going off all around her, from every direction. She could hear the Captain's orders being yelled out. Jolene curled into a ball and pulled her arms over her head, praying that Flint would come back to get her, only Flint!

"Is she alright, my friend?"

"Yes, at least I think so, she's finally fallen asleep."

"The danger is gone, does she know he is dead?"

Flint nodded at Paul, yes, he told her Awasos took a bullet. What he didn't tell her was that Paul shot the bastard. Flint would tell her later when she became calmer.

"She is a strong woman, she will be fine." Paul's hand gripped Flint's shoulder. "I must go."

"Yes, tell McKean we'll be there in a couple days."

"Oui, and I am leaving two strong men here to help you get the roof up tomorrow, then they will leave."

"You don't...."

"Yes, I do, he was my problem and I should have killed him the first time."

Flint met the man's hard gaze and nodded. He watched Paul leave before going into the house.

Jolene silently stood just inside the door. Her bottom lip quivered against the effort she used not to cry. "Oh Darlin'..." Flint opened his arms to take her to him. His large hand combed through the silken strands of her hair at the back of her head. "Cry Darlin', let it all come."

Her sobs rocked her whole body and Flint couldn't stand it. He gently picked her up in his arms and carried her over to the rocker he'd made for her to rock little Beth in.

"It's all right, Darlin', I'm here."

Her fingers gripped his arm and held on as if she'd fall if she let go and Flint rocked her and told her how he planned to build the dock she said they needed. And after a while, between hiccups she asked him if he could make her a cradle.

"Oh darlin, I already cut the wood for our son's cradle. You need to draw me a picture of the chair you talked about."

"And the playpen for Beth?"

Flint gently squeezed the woman in his arms. "Hmm, that too, should I make two?"

He smiled when she gave a small laugh and looked into her beautiful eyes. "I want lots of babies, Jolene."

"You better make two playpens then."

"Sure we shouldn't just build a bigger house and be done with it?"

He loved to watch her roll her eyes at him. His lips brushed her forehead to keep her from seeing the tears that filled his own.

When her hand came to rest on his cheek he turned and kissed her palm. "I…"

"Hush my love, I know…I know."

Jolene pushed herself up in his lap. She held his loving face in her hands and bent her head down to make him look at her. Her thumb wiped away the tear that rolled down his cheek. "It will be okay Allen, we are going to be fine. Besides we have to see this world grow and we have a lot to do for the children…"

His hungry lips silenced her words as he wrapped his arms around this marvelous woman. How she managed to turn herself around in his lap he couldn't say, but her legs wrapped around his waist, he pulled back and looked at her. "Jolene…are you…"

"Horny, oh my yes, for the man I love." She ran her tongue over his open lips. "Hmm, you taste so good, I want to feel you inside me Allen. I want you to drive that magnificent rod of yours into me until it fills me again and again." The kisses she planted on his lips weren't enough and Jolene drove her tongue into his mouth and gloried in the battle he gave her to take possession of her mouth, a battle she willingly lost. And as he worked on sliding her nightgown down her shoulders Jolene's hands worked on pulling apart the cords in his pants.

When she finally freed him neither of them bothered to move from the chair.

Jolene's eagerness to have him inside of her made her slide over the swollen head until his love drops lubricated her folds. "I want you Allen."

He guided her hips over the tip and slowly settled her over him, and she moaned in ecstasy as she took him inside. "Hmm, you feel so good."

Allen didn't answer, he was too busy tending to her breasts. "Ah woman you are so damn sweet!"

Jolene's hands were on his shoulders as she bent down and took hold of his mouth as she lowered herself over his length. Once she took him deep inside she deliberately contracted the wall of her womb around him, arousing him until he pulsed and jumped excitedly inside of her. And she pushed down further and moved over him, slowly pulling back and came back nice and easy to take him back inside until his hands started massaging her hips and urging her to move faster.

But Jolene wanted to have him inside of her for a long, long time. "Patience my love," she moved her breasts over his face, back and forth so his tongue could lick her nipples. "I came a long way to find you and I'm going to enjoy every second of our time together."

She smiled when Flint jerked up under her and drove in deeper. She knew he was letting her know he was ready to contribute whenever she wanted. In answer she move down in his lap, slipping away from him, then coming back she smoothed her body over his while she lowered her pussy back over that powerful shaft. Jolene kept this up as she tasted every marvelous inch of Allen's impressive body, her hands caressed and lovingly excited the man beneath her until she knew he couldn't take any more.

"Now Allen, oh yes, that's it...deeper Allen!"

"Anything for my Darlin.'"

Together they rode the crest of their passion until in throes of their climax they sealed the pinnacle of their love with a kiss driven in passion, sated in hungry love.

Jolene rolled over and into Allen's chest, her hand rested over the rushing beat of his heart. She smiled and kissed his heaving chest before snuggling closer, nothing seemed to satisfy her need for him. They shared many couplings this night and her body still quivered from her last climax.

She closed her eyes as his hand held her head to him, the way he touched her always made her feel so loved by this man.

"You are something really special Darlin.'" Her laughter tickled his chest. What she could do to him still surprised Flint, he'd never suspected it could be so thrilling to make love to a woman. "But then you are my wife...."

"Just think Allen, we're only just starting."

He could move so fast when he wanted. Jolene looked up at him as he loomed over her. She traced his bottom lip with the tip of her finger. He caught it and sucked on it taking it deep into his mouth.

"Sweet, like honey," He started kissing his way up her neck, "let's never stop, forever Jolene...through all time my Darlin.'"

T HE END

Don't miss out!

Visit the website below and you can sign up to receive emails whenever Jewel Adams publishes a new book. There's no charge and no obligation.

https://books2read.com/r/B-A-NXGC-XVVUB

BOOKS 2 READ

Connecting independent readers to independent writers.

Did you love *Darlin*? Then you should read *Falling In Time*[1] by Jewel Adams!

FALLING IN TIMEbyJewel AdamsSensual Romance Time Travel

Book 2 in the Loves in Time serie

Determined to be the Chicago Sun's top foreign reporter, Cassandra Malone is on her way to Riyadh. Cassie's adventure turns ugly when a group of terrorist highjack the jet. Gunfire fills the plane and bullets rip through the hull, Cassie's only thought is to survive the explosion. Captain Blaine Sterling's last voyage on the Stargazer is more profitable than he ever imagined when the ocean depths surrender a beautiful woman! Once given the gift, Blaine refuses to let death take the girl. The first time their gazes touch they both know their future is sealed. Together they face an adventure in love that takes them on a journey through the American wilderness of 1784. Cassie's modern knowledge might protect Blaine's thriving new settlement from the British allies, but can Blaine protect Cassie from the uncivilized frontier and the dangers lurking in every shadow. Falling in Time is a story of love that thrives despite all the

---

1. https://books2read.com/u/mqwNBZ

2. https://books2read.com/u/mqwNBZ

adversity thrown in its path. Don't miss this touching story of Cassie and Blaine's shared adventure in time.

Read more at https://authorjeweladams.godaddysites.com/.

Also by Jewel Adams

Loves In Time
Sails in Time
Falling In Time
Darlin
Dance in Time
Dream Lover
Gamble in Time
Answers In Time

Standalone
Savage Destiny
Do You Believe in Magic?

Watch for more at https://authorjeweladams.godaddysites.com/.

About the Author

The last few years have certainly seen changes for Jewel. An outstanding author of over 15 novels and novellas, she will be the first to tell you that the Romance genre is thriving on the internet. As an author, Jewel found the freedom to take her love of Romance beyond the established barriers. Danger, love, tears, and romance; Jewel's Erotic and sensual romance Time Travels, Gothic, Paranormal, Fantasy, Westerns, and Contemporary Romances will take you on thrilling journeys sparked with adventure, and fill your life with the love that can cross centuries and worlds. Be sure to look for her new releases and news at the following sites:

https://authorjeweladams.godaddysites.com/ https://author-jeweladams-lilysimmons.com/ http://www.facebook.com/jeweladams http://twitter.com/JewelAdams Email her at: jeweladams@gmail.com

Read more at https://authorjeweladams.godaddysites.com/.